Checkmate

The Conning Couple Series

Shane Reed

Copyright © 2024 by Shane Reed

All rights reserved.

No portion of this book may be reproduced in any form without written permission from the publisher or author, except as permitted by International copyright law.

CONTENTS

1. Chapter 1 — 1
2. Chapter 2 — 21
3. Chapter 3 — 37
4. Chapter 4 — 51
5. Chapter 5 — 68
6. Chapter 6 — 86
7. Chapter 7 — 100
8. Chapter 8 — 116
9. Chapter 9 — 138
10. Chapter 10 — 154
11. Acknowledgements — 162

Chapter 1

Subject: Seeking Vengeance and Justice

Dear Nathaniel,

I hope this email finds you well. My name is Evie, and I recently obtained your contact information from a mutual friend who spoke highly of your abilities in seeking justice and retribution for those who have been wronged. I am reaching out to you in desperate need of your expertise and assistance.

For the past few years, I have been working as a contracted cleaner for a company owned by Sebastian Blackwood. His company specializes in providing cleaning services for the lavish estates of wealthy individuals. Unfortunately, my experience working under Sebastian's employment has been nothing short of a nightmare.

To begin with, Sebastian has consistently underpaid me and, I suspect, many other staff members as well. The meager wages I receive are barely enough to provide for my toddler. As a single parent, I am left struggling to make ends meet, constantly living on the edge of financial instability.

However, the worst part of my ordeal is the degrading and humiliating treatment I have endured. One of Sebastian's clients coerced me into performing the cleaning duties naked.

During these instances, the homeowner pleasured himself while I carried out my job. Unfortunately word has spread amongst Sebastian's clients, and I was subsequently asked to continue performing these demeaning tasks by others. The tips I receive from these homeowners for this extra service only serve to marginally bring my income up to the level of minimum wage.

The disgust and shame I feel about having to resort to such degrading acts are overwhelming. I never imagined that I would find myself in a position where I would have to compromise my self-respect and dignity to provide for my child. It breaks my heart to think that I am forced to sell my body in such a way simply because I lack the skills necessary for alternative employment.

I have recently discovered that Sebastian is involved in fraudulent activities. He is running two sets of accounts, one for the taxman and another for his own personal gains. This revelation only adds to the injustice I have endured under his employment.

> *I implore you and your wife, Amy, to consider taking on my case. I firmly believe that you can bring justice to Sebastian Blackwood and expose his illegal activities.*
>
> *Your reputation as a modern-day A-Team duo, your history in hacking and conning wrongdoers, gives me hope that you can help me seek the vengeance and retribution I so desperately seek.*
>
> *Please let me know if you are able and willing to assist me in this matter. I am more than willing to provide any further information or meet with you in person to discuss the details of my situation.*
>
> *Time is of the essence, as every day that passes under Sebastian's rule feels like an eternity of suffering.*
>
> *Thank you for taking the time to read my plea. I eagerly await your response and hope that you can be the beacon of hope that my child and I desperately need.*
>
> *Sincerely,*
> *Evie*

Nathaniel "Nate" Everhart leaned back in his chair, a satisfied grin on his rugged face. Nate's skills as an ethical hacker had been honed during his time in the military, but it was his empathy for the vulnerable that drove him to use those skills for good.

His partner in both life and crime, Amelia "Amy" Everhart, sat at the opposite end of the room, her striking red hair cascading down her back as she peered at the documents scattered across the table. Her background in investigative journalism, combined with her razor-sharp attention to detail, made her an indispensable ally in their quest for justice. A survivor herself, Amy would go to hell and back to protect the innocent.

"Blackwood," Nate said, breaking the silence. "Sebastian Blackwood."

"Ah, yes," Amy replied, not looking up from her papers. "The man who makes Scrooge look like a philanthropist."

"Exactly," Nate chuckled, running a hand through his dark hair. "Someone needs our help."

Amy finally looked up, her green eyes flashing. "Tell me everything."

"I've just read in incoming email on Protonmail from a woman called Evie who has been doing work for him."

"What's with the air quotes when you said work?", Amy asked.

"Well, Sebastian 'Bastian' Blackwood," Nate began, rolling the name around his mouth like a bitter pill. "A wealthy business tycoon, pushing sixty. He's got his fingers in all sorts of pies, but his main gig seems to be outsourcing cleaning services to the rich and famous."

"Cleaning services? Sounds innocuous enough," Amy mused, arching an eyebrow.

"Appearances can be deceiving," Nate countered, his voice dropping to a conspiratorial whisper. "This guy seems to be making a fortune exploiting vulnerable people, Amy. He pays them a pittance and works them to the bone."

"That's what companies do, Nate. It's not called Human Resources for nothing. Anyone except the board are just resources. Human Resources."

"Yes, I know. The rich get richer. If people cost more to pay than they bring in, it's not a viable business. This is different though. This is someone who needs our help."

"You actually had me at someone needs our help. Spit it out, Nate."

"Better you read the email yourself, Hun. That way you have the same information as me."

Amy sauntered over to Nate's desk, her steps light and purposeful. She leaned in close, her hands resting on his broad shoulders as she peered curiously at the screen in front of him. Her delicate fingers traced the outline of his tense muscles, feeling the slight quiver beneath them. The scent of his cologne filled her nostrils, a familiar and comforting aroma that always made her heart skip a beat. She couldn't resist stealing a glance at his handsome profile, admiring the way his dark hair fell gracefully over his forehead. Their closeness sent a shiver down her spine, reminding her of all the moments they had shared just like this one, lost in each other's company.

Amy's jaw tightened. Her eyes narrowed as she finished reading. "So, what's our plan?"

"I haven't figured out a plan yet as such, but we need a 2 step process. Step 1: Find shit out about him; Step 2: Expose the shit."

"Sounds like an almost plan," Amy smirked. "We expose him for the heartless bastard he is, then, we make him pay – literally."

"Sounds closer to a plan," Nate agreed, a smile lighting up his face. "Let's get started."

Nate tapped on the "reply" button and began to type out a response. He sent Evie their contact information and assured her that they were willing to take on the case whenever she was ready.

***

Amy's fingers trembled as she hung up the phone.

She had just finished speaking with Evie and was left with a flurry of thoughts and emotions swirling in her head.

As Evie spoke, Amy frantically typed away. She needed to capture every detail - phone numbers, addresses, anything that could help her in this search.

Finally, she completed the form and saved it in the designated folder in the secure OneDrive vault.

Nate's fingers tapped furiously at the keyboard, his eyes darting back and forth as he delved into the digital underbelly of Sebastian Blackwood's businesses. He'd started with some careful Google Dorking, now he was running his well-used recon scripts in Kali Linux.

Amy sat across from him, her red hair reflecting the dim light of their makeshift office as she scrolled through pages of online news articles and records on her tablet.

"Listen to this," Amy said, her face scrunched in disgust. "Blackwood's cleaning company has a high turnover rate for employees, but most of them are too afraid to speak out about the working conditions. They're all financially struggling, just like Evie."

"Seems he only employs, targets, vulnerable females," Nate muttered, his jaw clenching with anger. "They're easier to manipulate and less likely to rock the boat."

"Exactly," Amy agreed. "And it looks like the naked cleaning gig isn't an isolated incident. There are anonymous posts on forums where others have mentioned similar experiences. They're just too scared to come forward officially."

Nate continued to search through the online records, his finger hovering over the mouse button as he considered the clues before him. Despite his anger, Nate was pretty good at what he did and knew that, if they were to make a case against Blackwood, they needed solid evidence.

He clicked on a link that took him to a page outlining employee salaries for Blackwood's cleaning service. It was much lower than the industry standard and it seemed that Evie was not the only one being underpaid. Nate could see why these women stayed quiet – there was no way they would be able to find another job if they spoke out against their employer. It's a big red flag to any interviewer. Inevitably all employees become ex employees at some time. If someone spoke bad of their previous employer during the interview, chances are they would speak bad about them when they're interviewing for their next job. That's a risk. No-one wants bad press.

"Got something," Nate announced triumphantly after a few more minutes of digging. "Blackwood siphons off extra profits from his cleaning business by underpaying his employees and pocketing the difference. He keeps two sets of books – one for the taxman and another for himself."

"Can you, what's the word you use? Obtain? Can you 'obtain' those?" Amy asked, her eyes widening as she realized the potential impact of their discovery.

"Already on it," Nate replied, his fingers flying faster than ever. Nate was quiet, frantically working, for a few minutes before breaking the silence. "Dumbass. Password wasn't his password, I mean, it might have been once, but it's now Password1. Idiot should use Multi Factor Authentication too"

It wasn't long before Nate had complete access to all of Blackwood's data. Blackwood had used the same password. It's simple: Get one password and try it somewhere else. Credential stuffing is a real thing. A stupid idea unless you want strangers getting access to your data; a great thing if you are the one wanting access to the data. "People are funnier than anybody", Nate thought.

"This goes deeper than we first thought, Amy. He's not just scamming his employees; he's stealing from the clients, too. Padding the bills for cleaning services and pocketing the extra cash."

"Unbelievable," Amy shook her head in disbelief. "The extent of his greed knows no bounds. But this is exactly what we need. Concrete proof of his misdeeds."

"Right," Nate nodded, his voice filled with determination. "And now that we have it, we can use it to bring him down – for Evie, and for all the others he's hurt."

Amy reached out to squeeze Nate's hand, her eyes blazing with resolve. "We're going to make sure Blackwood pays for what he's done. And more importantly, we'll make sure Evie gets the justice she deserves."

"Darn Tooting," Nate agreed, his voice echoing the same ferocity.

"Literally nobody says Darn Tooting, Nate"

"My Grandmother did," Nate replied.

It hadn't taken too long. They had uncovered the evidence they needed to expose Sebastian Blackwood's exploitation and bring him to justice. And neither of them would rest until they saw it through.

Nate stared into the distance, picturing the countless people that had been taken advantage of by Blackwood. He clenched his fists, feeling a surge of protectiveness that sent a shiver down his spine. Beside him, Amy shared the same fierce determination to right the wrongs committed against them.

"Can you believe someone would exploit others like that?" Amy asked, her voice shaking with anger. "Forcing people like Evie to degrade herself just to make ends meet? It's disgusting."

"Unfortunately, I can," Nate replied darkly, his mind flashing back to his military days when he had witnessed firsthand how ruthless some could be in their pursuit of power. "But that doesn't mean we have to accept it. We're going to put a stop to Blackwood's twisted game, no matter the cost."

Amy nodded, her red hair cascading over her shoulders as she leaned forward, her green eyes locked onto his. "We need to take this case, Nate. I know it won't be easy – Blackwood is well-connected and dangerous because he's connected – but we have to do whatever it takes to help Evie and others like her."

"That's right," Nate agreed firmly, his jaw set in determination. "Blackwood has made a lot of enemies though during his rise to power, it's only a matter of time before someone exposes him. But if we don't act soon, who knows how many more people will suffer before that happens?"

"So let's do it," Amy declared, her gaze unwavering. "Let's take on this case and bring Blackwood to justice. We've faced risks and challenges before, and we've always come out on top. We can do this."

Nate laced his fingers through hers, drawing strength from the warmth of her touch. "You're right, we can do this. And we will. For Evie, for all the other victims, and for ourselves. We need to show Blackwood that he can't continue to exploit people without consequences."

"Yes," Amy agreed, a fiery glint in her eyes as they shared a moment of unspoken understanding. They both knew the risks involved in taking on someone as powerful and dangerous as Sebastian Blackwood, but they also knew that they couldn't stand by while innocent people suffered.

"Back to work," Nate said, his voice filled with resolve. Together, they would face whatever challenges lay ahead, determined to bring justice to the victims and expose the full extent of Blackwood's vile exploitation.

Nate couldn't help but smile. For all the darkness and danger that awaited them, there was something almost exhilarating about diving headfirst into the unknown, armed only with their wits and each other. Side by side, they would face whatever the world threw at them – and emerge stronger for it.

Nate leaned back in his chair, studying the array of digital files and photographs spread across their large computer screen. Beside him, Amy tapped a pen against her chin, her eyes narrowed as she scrutinized every piece of information they had gathered on Sebastian Blackwood. Despite the enormity of the task ahead, Nate felt a surge of confidence running through him, fueled by the knowledge that together, they were an almost unstoppable force.

"Piece of cake, right?" he teased, nudging Amy with his elbow. "We've taken down bigger fish than this."

"True," Amy agreed, smirking at her husband's bravado. "But we can't afford to underestimate Blackwood. He didn't get where he is by being careless."

"I guess you're right," Nate said, his tone more serious now. "But we've got the perfect blend of skills to expose him. It's like we were made for this."

"Sure," Amy nodded, her gaze fixed on a photograph of Blackwood shaking hands with a well-known politician. "Now we just need to find a way in."

"Which means we'll need a cover story," Nate mused, steepling his fingers as he considered their options. "Something that'll give us access to his inner circle without raising suspicions."

"Ah, yes – the inevitable false credentials," Amy said, tapping the pen against her lips thoughtfully. "We could pose as wealthy investors looking to partner with one of Blackwood's companies."

"Blackwood may be a scumbag, but he's no fool," Nate remarked, rubbing his chin. "He'll have people checking up on us. We'll need a solid backstory that can withstand scrutiny."

"Okay," Amy admitted. "Fortunately, that's something we're rather good at."

Nate grinned, recalling past operations where they'd successfully infiltrated high society, befriended dangerous criminals, and even impersonated royalty. "Let's make it interesting this time," he suggested. "How about we're newlyweds – rich, philanthropic, and looking to invest in a company with a strong social conscience?"

"Ah, the perfect bait for a man like Blackwood," Amy chuckled, her eyes sparkling with mischief. "We'll need some convincing documentation – passports, bank statements, maybe even a fake wedding album."

"Leave that to me," Nate promised, his fingers already flying across the keyboard and swishing the mouse as he began crafting their new identities. "The AI in Photoshop should make the wedding album a breeze. By the time I'm done, we'll be the most eligible couple on the East Coast."

As they built out their cover story, Nate couldn't help but feel a thrill at the prospect of taking down Sebastian Blackwood. He loved that feeling, that high, that sense of danger during the operation, the risk of getting caught out, and accomplishment when the mission was a success. They had faced difficult challenges before, but each time they had emerged victorious, their bond stronger than ever. No resting on laurels though, Nate knew that each time they pulled a stunt the odds against them increased and it could be their last. They needed to be thorough.

***

A few days had passed since Nate and Amy had begun working on their cover story and creating the necessary documents to support it. Now, they found themselves lounging in the plush living room of their longtime friend, Artie Matthews. Artie was a man who knew how to make connections, and his extensive network of influential acquaintances would be invaluable for infiltrating Sebastian Blackwood's world.

"So, what brings you two to my humble abode?" Artie asked, popping open a bottle of champagne and pouring three glasses. He handed one to each of them before sinking into a leather armchair.

"We need your help," Nate said, taking a sip of the bubbly liquid. "We're looking to get close to Sebastian Blackwood – the businessman slash philanthropist slash criminal mastermind."

Artie raised an eyebrow. "That's quite a goal you've set for yourselves. What can I do to assist?"

"We need introductions," Amy replied. "We're thinking of posing as wealthy investors looking to partner with one of Blackwood's companies."

"Ah, yes – that would explain all the wedding talk I've been hearing from Nate," Artie chuckled.

"Exactly," Nate grinned. "We want to create some buzz around our fabricated personas."

Artie leaned forward, intrigued by their plan. "I do have some connections in high society that could be useful for this operation," he said thoughtfully.

"That would be incredible," Amy exclaimed with excitement.

"But there is one condition," Artie added, his expression turning serious.

Nate and Amy exchanged glances, already anticipating what Artie might ask for in return for his help.

"We'll owe you one," Nate stated confidently. He knew that whatever favor Artie asked for, they would be more than willing to pay it back tenfold.

"Amy will sing at my charity gala next month," Artie said with a smile.

Nate and Amy both laughed in relief. Amy was a skilled singer. Nate loved listening to her sing. Her voice was like a quivering flame, full of passion and emotion, and her every note was a burst of color that painted the air around her. To Nate, her singing was like a full body hug.

Nate smiled at Artie. "We need to get close enough to gather evidence and expose his exploitation of his staff. One woman, Evie, in particular."

Artie nodded, understanding the gravity of the situation. He leaned forward, elbows resting on his knees. "Leave it to me. I'll introduce you as the charming and successful couple you are – or at least, pretend to be." His jovial tone belied the seriousness with which he approached their mission.

"Thank you, Artie," Amy said gratefully, reaching out to squeeze her friend's hand. "We couldn't do this without you."

"Of course not," Artie replied, smirking. "After all, who else could pull off such an elaborate ruse?"

As they discussed the finer details of their cover story and planned introductions to influential individuals, Nate felt a familiar thrill coursing through him. They had faced seemingly impossible odds before, but every time, they managed to come out on top.

"Once we've ingratiated ourselves with Blackwood, we can do some deeper digging," Nate said, his voice low and determined. "We'll find the proof we need to bring him down."

Amy's eyes mirrored his resolve, a fierce fire burning within them. "For Evie," she whispered, her voice laced with both conviction and empathy.

"Absolutely," Nate replied, reaching for her hand. "For Evie, yes. But also for all the other people Blackwood has trodden on."

Together, they were about to embark on yet another mission to right the wrongs in their world. Nate looked into Amy's eyes. Regardless of what challenges lay ahead, they would face them head-on – and they would win.

***

Back at home, the dining room was a controlled chaos of research materials, maps, and notes – all essential pieces to the intricate puzzle they were about to solve. A gust of wind blew through the open window, ruffling the stack of printouts on the table.

"Alright, I think we've got everything," Nate said, his voice steady and filled with purpose. He adjusted his glasses and looked through the pile of papers, ensuring nothing had been overlooked.

Amy nodded in agreement, her red hair shimmering in the sunlight that streamed through the window. "We've got our cover story, Artie's connections, and a detailed understanding of Blackwood's businesses. Now we just need to put the plan into motion."

She clenched her fists in the anticipation of facing Sebastian Blackwood. Amy knew there would be risks, but she couldn't wait to see the look on Blackwood's face when they exposed him for what he truly was – a callous exploiter of vulnerable individuals like Evie.

Nate reached out and placed a reassuring hand on Amy's shoulder. "Hey, remember, deep breaths. We've done this before, and we'll do it again."

Amy smiled at Nate. "Pride comes before a fall."

Nate looked down at his feet. "My laces are tied. I'm not going to trip on them. I'm not falling and I won't be failing."

Amy beamed at her husband, grateful for his unwavering support. They had faced daunting challenges together in the past, but their shared determination to bring justice to those who needed it most had always propelled them forward.

"Once we're in Blackwood's circle, we'll gather as much evidence as we can without arousing suspicion," Nate explained, his eyes scanning the pages of their meticulously crafted plan. "Then we'll make our move."

"Exactly. And once we expose him, everyone will know the truth," Amy added, her thoughts drifting to Evie and the countless others who had suffered at the hands of people like Blackwood.

"Can you imagine the look on Blackwood's face when his world comes crashing down around him?" Nate mused with a wicked grin, momentarily allowing himself a moment of levity. "I'd pay good money to see that."

"Me too," Amy agreed, chuckling softly. "But first, we need to make sure everything is in place."

"Right," Nate replied, his focus back on their mission. He looked over the documents one last time, double-checking their preparations and ensuring they had every possible advantage going into this operation.

"We need to do this," Nate announced, determination etched across his face. "Not just for Evie, but for everyone else who's been wronged by Blackwood."

"Absolutely," Amy agreed, her eyes blazing with resolve. "Let's get some justice." Amy glanced at Nate with the smirk that she knew he adored.

Nate glanced at the clock. "I'm with you, but it's a bit late, Hun. We'll have to pick up on this in the morning. Nothing more can be achieved tonight, everyone else in this town is asleep. We should be too."

Chapter 2

"Alright, Hun," Nate began, his dark eyes gleaming with determination as he leaned in across the small table. "We need to gather some solid evidence against Blackwood. It's time we put an end to his exploitation and embezzlement."

Amy nodded, her red hair cascading down her back as she tapped her pen on a notepad filled with scribbled notes. "I think we've seen what he's capable of doing. Evie deserves justice, and we need to make that happen."

"Darn tootin'." Nate laughed, cracked his knuckles and opened his laptop, ready to dive into the depths of Blackwood's business dealings. "Let's start by figuring out how he's connected to Evie's financial struggles."

"Right behind you, partner," Amy said, half-smiling as she focused on her research.

For the next few hours, Nate and Amy delved into the intricate web of Blackwood's businesses, from his outsourcing cleaning services to his investments in real estate. They painstakingly cross-referenced transactions and contracts, determined to find the link between the tycoon's wealth and the hardships of his staff.

"Look at this, Nate," Amy said, pointing to a series of transactions on her screen. "Blackwood's company has been underpaying its employees – Evie included – for years. No wonder she couldn't make ends meet."

"Unbelievable," Nate muttered, anger bubbling inside him. But it wasn't just the unfair wages; they soon discovered that many employees were forced to perform extra favors for clients just to earn extra tips to survive. Naked cleaning while the clients pleasured themselves was probably the tip of the iceberg.

"Blackwood's got them trapped in this vicious cycle," Amy said, her voice barely concealing her disgust. "We need to find a way to break it."

Nate couldn't help but chuckle at his wife's unwavering resolve. "You know what they say, 'Behind every great man is a woman rolling her eyes.'"

"Ha!" Amy snorted, shaking her head. "That's us, alright." Amy rolled her eyes dramatically. "Now let's keep digging. We're bound to find something we can use against him."

Nate sighed. "It seems like the more we uncover, the angrier I get. How can this guy sleep at night knowing he's taking advantage of vulnerable people?"

"Money? They're just pawns. Believe me, Nate, my blood is boiling too," Amy replied, her face flushed with anger. She sighed and leaned back in her chair, running a hand through her fiery red hair. "But getting angry won't help. We need to focus on gathering solid evidence."

Nate sighed in agreement, then took a deep breath to calm himself. He stared at the screen before him, his thoughts racing. "We have to be smart about this. If we charge in without a plan, we risk alerting this bastard or putting others in danger."

Amy's eyes narrowed as she considered their options. "We need to think several steps ahead, anticipate his moves, and stay one step ahead of him."

"Exactly," Nate said, rubbing his chin thoughtfully. "I could try to access Blackwood's financial records and look for any incriminating transactions. People like him will always fall for a nicely crafted phishing email. We'll also need to find evidence of the exploitation directly affecting Evie and the other employees."

Amy nodded. "We'll need to speak with some of the clients and other employees, gather their stories. But do it discreetly. We don't want to raise any suspicions."

"Good idea," Nate said, a mischievous glint in his eyes. "We could pose as prospective clients looking to hire Blackwood's cleaning services, that way we can get close to both the clients and the employees without arousing suspicion."

"Perfect," Amy grinned, feeling a spark of excitement despite the gravity of the situation. "We can use our charm to get them talking."

"Speaking of charm," Nate teased, "I'll have to make sure I don't get too carried away. We wouldn't want anyone falling head over heels for me now, would we?"

"Ha! When I said "we", I meant me. You just make sure you don't use your charms on Blackwood himself," Amy retorted with an eye-roll, a welcome moment of levity breaking through the tension.

"Deal," Nate laughed, his focus returning to their plan. "Alright, let's do a bit more recon. We need to figure out the best way to approach the clients and employees without tipping off Blackwood."

"Sounds like a plan," Amy agreed.

***

The sun dipped low in the sky, casting an orange glow over Blackwood's upscale offices, which Nate and Amy could see from where they had set up their stakeout. They sat in their somewhat unassuming sedan, dressed as a well-to-do couple looking for cleaning services for their opulent home. Nate adjusted his tie, a slight smirk on his lips as he caught sight of himself in the rearview mirror.

"Looking good, Mr. Everhart," Amy teased, straightening her blazer. "Now remember, we're here to gather intel, not win a fashion show."

"Of course, my dear," Nate replied with a wink. "Operation: Clean House is officially underway."

They spent some time conducting discreet interviews with anyone leaving Blackwood's offices that would be willing to talk. Posing as potential customers doing their due diligence allowed them to talk to both clients and employees. Their resourcefulness and adaptability allowed them to slip seamlessly into character, eliciting stories of mistreatment and financial ruin from those who had crossed paths with Blackwood.

As noon passed and the shadows grew longer, they found themselves speaking with a former employee named Maria. Her account was particularly harrowing; she had just been fired without warning after asking for time off to care for her sick child. With no income and mounting medical bills, Maria's family faced eviction and homelessness.

Nate clenched his jaw, feeling a surge of anger at Blackwood's cruelty. "This is beyond despicable," he muttered under his breath, staring intently at the modest house before them. "Blackwood is destroying lives left and right, all for his own greed."

Amy nodded, her eyes filled with empathy. "We can't let him continue to exploit them like this."

Nate nodded, determination etching itself across his face. "Our main priority is still Evie, but we'll do everything we can to bring justice to everyone Blackwood has wronged."

"Speaking of evidence," Nate said, pulling out his phone and tapping away at the screen. "I think I've found something interesting." He showed Amy a series of transactions between Blackwood's company and an offshore account, each one coinciding with a sudden increase in fees for his clients. "This could be the smoking gun we need to prove his exploitation."

Amy let out a low whistle, his eyes widening in disbelief as he scrolled through the damning records. "Nice work, Hubby. This is definitely going to help our case."

"Let's just hope it's enough," Nate murmured, his expression somber as he thought of all the pain and suffering Blackwood had caused.

They were weaving through the lives of those affected by Blackwood's greed and their resolve only grew stronger with each discovery. The emotional impact of each story fueled their determination to expose Blackwood's wrongdoing and bring him to justice once and for all. With each new piece of evidence they collected, they felt more confident in their mission, and more committed to ensuring that Evie and others like her would finally have their day in court.

"Blackwood won't know what hit him," Nate said, his voice filled with quiet fury as they drove away from their final interview of the day.

Amy grinned, her fire returning as she gripped the steering wheel. "We're going to make sure he pays for what he's done, and we'll do it with style."

"Style?" Nate chuckled, raising an eyebrow. "Well, we do look rather dashing in these outfits, don't you think?"

"Focus, Hun," Amy laughed, swatting him playfully on the arm. "We still have a long way to go, but we're one step closer to bringing the bastard down, and that's worth celebrating."

Nate ran a hand through his dark hair, frustration etched on his face as he stared at the piles of evidence spread across the table.

"We have to be smart about this. If we go in guns blazing, so to speak, we could end up putting the staff in danger."

Amy nodded, her red hair catching the dim light from the lamp. She traced her finger along the edge of a photograph, deep in thought. "You're right. We need to consider all the potential risks and consequences before we make our move. Blackwood is no fool. He's been doing this for years, and he knows how to cover his tracks."

"Exactly," Nate agreed. "We need to be certain that we gather evidence without alerting him or any of his cronies. That's easier said than done, though." He leaned back in his chair, rubbing his temples as he grappled with the enormity of their task.

Amy tapped her pen against her notebook, her green eyes narrowed in determination. "What if we split up? Divide and conquer, you know? You could focus on hacking more into Blackwood's financials, while I handle the interviews and surveillance."

"Splitting up could work," Nate mused, considering their options. "But we need to be careful. If either of us gets caught snooping around, it's endex."

"Endex?"

"Sorry, military term. If we get caught snooping about, it'll be game over"

"Then we'll just have to be extra cautious," Amy replied, "we've faced dangerous situations before, and we've always come out on top. This is no different."

"True," Nate admitted, a grin tugging at the corner of his mouth. "Remember that time in Paris when you pretended to be a mime to distract that group of thieves? That was something else."

"Hey, it worked, didn't it?" Amy laughed, her eyes sparkling with mischief. "Same here. We need to think outside the box and use our strengths to our advantage."

"So, let's make a plan," Nate said. "I'll start by snooping around Blackwood's financial records without raising suspicion. You can start mapping out and researching the key players and the best locations for surveillance."

"Sounds good," Amy replied, already scrolling through her phone to pull up a list of potential contacts. "Once we have all the evidence we need, we can reconvene and decide on the best course of action."

Nate clapped his hands together and cracked his knuckles. "Blackwood won't know what hit him."

Nate's fingers danced across the keyboard like a seasoned pianist. It was a bit cramped working in the car, having only one screen, but it worked. His mind was a whirlwind of calculations and connections. He loved the buzz. He loved that others thought hacking was part of an intricate dance, gracefully sidestepping firewalls and evading detection with ease. The truth was far less like Hollywood portrayed it to be though. More often than not, people used a guessable password ... and then, crazily, used that same password for multiple sites. Because they used the same password on multiple sites, all Nate had to do was grab one set of their credentials to any site from the dark web and see if they worked on their other accounts that he needed access to. Sometimes he had a bit of a setback if they used MFA, Multi Factor Authentication, but that was easily enough to bypass with some crafty social engineering. A quick phone call with a plausible story was all that was needed. People are the weakest link in any security system.

"Got it," he whispered triumphantly, his voice barely audible in the dimly lit room. "I've found a series of, let's call them questionable, transactions that seem to be linked to Evie's financial struggles."

"Great work," Amy responded, her gaze never leaving the building across the street. Her red hair was tucked under a dark baseball cap, and she held a pair of binoculars steady in her hands. Through the lens, she observed the comings and goings of people who looked far too ordinary to be involved in Blackwood's illicit activities. Yet she knew better than to underestimate appearances. "We're getting closer."

"Any luck on your end?" Nate asked, momentarily glancing up from his screens.

"Nothing concrete yet, but there's a pattern emerging," Amy said, her voice tense with concentration. "Blackwood seems to have several key players who frequent this location, and I'm starting to put faces to names."

"Perfect," Nate muttered, his attention already back on the digital labyrinth before him. "The more we know about Blackwood's network, the easier it will be to navigate it and gather evidence."

Amy peered at the building through her binoculars one last time.

"Looks like nothing more going on here," she said eventually. "Let's move out."

"Ok," Nate replied.

Nate had a few leads to follow up on, but he also wanted to get some rest before they launched their next attack on Blackwood's network. Taking a deep breath, he focused his attention back on the road ahead of them and pressed down firmly on the accelerator. It was time to get back to work – but this time from a safer distance.

CHECKMATE

Nate and Amy retreated to their makeshift headquarters, a disheveled apartment above a now-defunct Chinese restaurant. It wasn't anything to write home about, but it served a purpose and, more importantly, it was free. Artie "Knew someone who knew someone" and had been able to borrow the keys. The scent of soy sauce and stale fortune cookies lingered in the air.

Nate glanced at Amy with a wry smile. "Maybe we should've called ourselves 'The Fortune Cookie Avengers' instead."

Amy chuckled, her eyes sparkling with amusement. "I can just see you in a superhero costume."

"Yeah, I think you'd look a lot better in a tight costume", Nate quipped.

"Check this out," Nate said, opening a folder in Blackwood's cloud drive called 'Blackmail pictures'.

It had photos of several different people wiping or dusting. Some of them were topless, some were fully nude. There were different women, not just Evie.

"The homeowners were secretly taking photos or video and sending them to Blackwood", Nate thought aloud. "Blackwood knew that's what his staff were doing. No doubt he showed the photos to potential clients to help swing the deal. His customers all sent their pictures to him in exchange for the pictures from his other clients. Look, he's got a folder for which ones come from where and which ones have gone out to who."

"This is huge." Amy tapped one of the pictures thoughtfully. "We knew he was exploiting Evie and others like her, but this goes beyond anything we could've imagined."

"Careful where you're tapping, Ames", Nate said, raising an eyebrow. "That's Evie's butt. I didn't know you were Bi."

"Aren't we all? Really? Deep down?", Amy teased.

"Speak for yourself, Hon. Not my thing. Your sexual fantasies aside, we can't let him get away with this. We have to make sure that the people he's hurt get justice."

"Yeah, power to the people" Amy declared with a smile, raising her fist and looking up. Her red hair fell into her face. She brushed it back impatiently, then looked up at Nate with a mischievous grin. "You know, if we ever decide to give up our life of conning crime-fighters, we'd make an excellent team of private investigators."

"Or maybe food critics," Nate replied, smirking. "But first things first: the operation at hand."

"Right," Amy said, her expression turning serious. "I enjoying working together like this."

"Me too," Nate admitted, his voice tinged with affection. "There's no one else I'd rather have by my side."

"Same here," Amy said, her eyes shining with love and trust.

CHECKMATE

***

Nate and Amy crouched behind a row of bushes, their breaths shallow and quiet as they observed the imposing Blackwood estate in front of them. The late-night moon cast long shadows across the manicured lawn, giving their hiding spot just enough cover to remain unseen.

Heavy droplets of rain fell from the dark sky, pattering against the ground and leaving shiny puddles in their wake. The leaves on the nearby bushes were glistening with water, illuminated by the faint light of the moon.

This was the best weather for cat burglars. The rain stopped people getting a good view, creating reasonable doubt. If they were looking through a window, passing in their car for instance, all they really saw was the raindrops on the glass.

"Remember," Amy whispered, her voice barely audible, "we're looking for documents linking Blackwood to Evie's debt. Once we have that, we can expose him for the exploitative scumbag he is. Anything useful really that we haven't found on his cloud drive."

Nate nodded, his jaw set with determination. He glanced over at Amy, her fiery red hair almost glowing in the moonlight. "You ready?"

"I was born ready," she replied, a hint of humor in her eyes despite the serious situation.

With a final deep breath, they darted out from the bushes and approached the side entrance of the mansion. Nate quickly reached into his pocket and pulled out a screwdriver and a set of bump keys, normal keys that had the cuts shaved down. He quickly sorted through the keys to find the one that matched the lock brand. He put the bump key into the lock, gave it a tap with the handle of the screwdriver and twisted the key to open the door. Bumping locks was so much easier than picking them.

The interior of Blackwood's mansion was as grand as one would expect, filled with priceless artwork and opulent furnishings. However, Nate and Amy had no time to appreciate the decor; they moved silently through the halls, looking for Blackwood's office where they were sure they'd find something that could prove useful.

As they crossed the threshold of a doorway, a soft creak echoed through the hallway. Nate froze in place, his heart pounding in his chest. Amy shot him a worried look, her eyes wide with concern as they listened for any signs of discovery. For a tense moment, they stood motionless, waiting.

When nothing else stirred, Nate let out a silent sigh of relief and gestured for Amy to follow. They continued down the hall, their footsteps light and barely audible on the plush carpeting.

"Next time," Nate thought, "I'm definitely investing in some quieter shoes."

Finally, they found Blackwood's office, its heavy oak door standing imposingly before them. Nate carefully turned the handle and pushed it open, revealing a lavish room filled with leather-bound books and a massive desk.

The scent of cigar smoke hung heavy in the air, musky and sweet with hints of earthy tobacco and a hint of spice.

"Alright," Amy whispered, her eyes scanning the room, "let's find those documents and get out of here."

As they rifled through drawers and cabinets, Nate couldn't help but feel a growing sense of anger towards Blackwood and his exploitation of Evie. Each piece of evidence they uncovered only confirmed the depths of his greed and callousness.

Suddenly, a muffled sound echoed from main entrance. They heard the door shut and indistinct voices. Nate and Amy exchanged panicked glances, realizing that someone was in the house. They needed to act fast.

"Got it," Amy hissed, triumphantly holding up a folder filled with incriminating paperwork. "No time to copy it, we need to snatch it and see if we can return it later." Nate nodded, his mind racing as he formulated an escape plan.

They slipped through the door of the office, Amy pulled the door to as ajar as it was when they entered. Swiftly they reached the main living room, there was an impressively large painting above the fireplace but no time to appreciate it. Whoever had come through the front door could be heading to the study but, just as likely, they could be heading to the main living room.

The key was in the door to the French doors. "So trusting," thought Nate. He unlocked the door and turned the handle. Thank heavens for Cedar wood. It doesn't expand and contract as much as other woods. The door opened easily, allowing their silent escape.

The tension in their bodies slowly dissipated as they put distance between themselves and the Blackwood estate.

"Bit too close for comfort," Amy said approached the car.

"Danger is my middle name," Nate replied as though he had a plum in his throat.

"Alright, Austin Powers," Amy laughed.

"Austin 'Danger' Powers," Nate quipped.

Chapter 3

Nate Everhart leaned back in his swivel chair, sipping a glass of whiskey as he studied the blueprint on the screen. Beside him, Amelia "Amy" Everhart sat at her own computer, her striking red hair pulled back into a messy bun, and her piercing green eyes reflecting the light from her monitor.

"Alright, here's what I'm thinking," Nate began, setting down his glass with determination. "For the take down of Bastian, we change the cover story being high-profile consultants. It'll give us access to some key players and allow us to gather intel without raising suspicion."

Amy nodded thoughtfully, sensing the strategic edge to their plan. "That could work, but it might need a bit more groundwork. We need to be convincing."

"Leave that to me," Nate said with a charismatic grin. His intelligence and ability to read people had always been his greatest strengths. "First, we'll need to build our online presence – LinkedIn profiles, websites, references, the works. Then, we start networking. We get ourselves introduced to the right people."

As he outlined the steps, Amy's attention to detail kicked in. She started typing up a list of tasks they would need to accomplish, her fingers flying across the keyboard. Her adaptability and quick thinking were invaluable when it came to implementing their plans.

"Okay, so I'll research the industry to make sure we're using the right terminology and hitting the right pain points," Amy offered, adding the task to their growing to-do list. "Meanwhile, you can work on creating our digital personas. Make sure everything looks legit, from our education to our work experience."

"Done," Nate agreed, already opening new browser tabs to begin the process. Despite the weightiness of their mission, a glint of amusement shone in his eyes. He'd always enjoyed hacking for fun and found satisfaction in using his skills for a noble cause.

"Once we've established our credentials, it's time to put on a show," Nate continued, rubbing his hands together with excitement. "We attend a few conferences, make some connections, and before long, we'll be in the inner circle."

"Sounds like a plan," Amy said, her eyes narrowing as she focused on her research. She would do anything to protect those who had been wronged, just as she'd fought for her father when he was falsely accused.

Nate raised his glass in a toast. "To us – the Everharts, masters of deception and seekers of justice."

Amy grinned and clinked her own glass against his. "May our cover story be as convincing as our love is true."

***

The next morning, Nate and Amy woke with renewed vigor. The sun cast a golden hue over the city, as if to bless their endeavors. Nate's mind raced with thoughts of their plan while Amy's hand rested reassuringly on his arm.

"Let's pay Artie a visit," Nate suggested, making a quick decision. "We could use some help from a man like him."

"Good idea," Amy agreed, already pulling up Artie's contact information on her phone.

Artie Matthews was a loyal friend who had known Nate since their college days. With silver hair that always seemed perfectly combed and tailored suits that fit him like a second skin, he exuded sophistication and success. Artie's connections and influence were legendary among their circle, and he'd maintained those relationships through his charm and genuine warmth.

Nate pressed the call button on Amy's phone, holding it between them so they could both speak into the receiver. A few rings later, Artie's smooth voice filled their ears.

"Ah, the Everharts!" Artie greeted them cheerfully. "To what do I owe the pleasure?"

"Hey, Artie," Nate responded, grinning despite the seriousness of their mission. "We could use your help."

"Of course," Artie replied without hesitation. "What do you need?"

Nate and Amy glanced at each other, exchanging a look that conveyed both their excitement and determination. Then, Nate launched into an explanation of their plan: creating a cover story as high-profile consultants in order to infiltrate an organization and right a terrible wrong.

"Sounds like quite the undertaking," Artie mused after Nate finished explaining, "a better ruse for the attack than newlyweds. That worked for the initial recon, but I figured you'd change the scenario for next phase. What kind of credentials are you trying to establish? How can I help?"

"Thanks, Artie," Amy interjected, her voice soft yet firm. "We need to create believable backgrounds in our chosen fields – something that will hold up under scrutiny. We're thinking Nate could pose as a cybersecurity expert, while I take on the role of a communications specialist."

"Interesting choices, and not too far from the truth, so it should be easy for you to talk the talk," Artie remarked thoughtfully. "I think I can help with that. Let me make some calls and see what I can come up with. Just leave it to me."

"Thanks, Artie," Nate said, relief washing over him. "We knew we could count on you."

"Always, my friend," Artie replied warmly. "Just remember to return the favor someday."

"Oh it'll be more than a song or two," Nate agreed, his voice laced with both gratitude and anticipation. They were one step closer to making their plan a reality, and with Artie's help, they knew they had a fighting chance at success.

Artie leaned back in his plush leather chair, a wry smile playing on his lips as he regarded Nate and Amy. "You two have always had a knack for walking the line between brilliance and sheer insanity," he said, chuckling softly. "There's something about this plan of yours that feels... right."

"Thank you, Artie," Amy said, relief evident in her voice. "Your help means everything to us."

"Of course," Artie replied, his eyes twinkling with excitement. He glanced down at the notes he'd taken during their conversation and began to mentally map out the steps he would need to take in order to create convincing credentials for his friends. The game was afoot, and Artie Matthews was more than ready to play.

***

Over the next few days, Artie immersed himself in the world of cybersecurity and communications, meticulously researching the intricate details of each field. He reached out to old acquaintances and leveraged his extensive network of connections to gather information, always careful to maintain an air of casual curiosity.

"Ah, yes," he would say, feigning nonchalance as he traced looping patterns onto the surface of his mahogany desk, phone cradled against his ear. "I'm looking into hiring some top-notch consultants for a project I'm working on, you see. Just want to make sure I know what to look for."

In between phone calls and googling, Artie took the time to craft impressive Search Engine Optimized résumés for Nate and Amy, skillfully weaving together bits of truth and fiction like an expert tapestry-maker.

"Look at these," Artie marveled as he handed the freshly printed pages over to Nate and Amy. "Nathaniel Everhart: cybersecurity consultant extraordinaire, with an emphasis on ethical hacking and a background in the military. Amelia Everhart: communications specialist, boasting a storied career in investigative journalism."

"Artie, these are excellent," Nate said, his eyes scanning the text with a mix of awe and gratitude. "How did you manage all this?"

"Trade secret," Artie replied, tapping his nose conspiratorially. "Let's just say I've learned a thing or two about spinning a good yarn over the years. Now, let's talk strategy."

As they delved into the specifics of their plan, Nate marvelled at the ease with which Artie had crafted their identities. It was as if he'd breathed life into characters, their stories unfolding before them like the pages of a well-worn novel. And with each carefully chosen detail, each expertly placed connection, Nate could feel the weight of their mission growing lighter.

"Are you sure you don't want to join us, Artie?" Amy asked suddenly, her eyes dancing with mischief. "We could use someone with your skills on the inside."

"Ah, my dear," Artie replied, laughing warmly. "I'm afraid my talents are best suited to the shadows. But rest assured, I'll be cheering you both on from the sidelines."

"Thanks, Artie," Nate said, clapping his friend on the shoulder. "We couldn't do this without you."

"Remember that when it's time for payback," Artie teased.

Artie settled into his plush leather chair, the low hum of his mahogany desk phone providing a familiar soundtrack as he dialed number after number. Nate and Amy sat across from him, watching intently as their friend worked his magic.

"Ralph, old buddy!" Artie boomed, speaking to a powerful CEO he'd known for years. "I've got two people here you absolutely must meet. They're extraordinary consultants who are about to revolutionize the industry. Trust me, you'll want them on your side." Artie winked at Nate and Amy, an air of mischief in his eyes.

Nate and Amy exchanged a glance before launching into their practiced pitch, highlighting their unique qualifications and past successes. As they spoke, Artie felt a sense of pride and satisfaction. He had helped create these impressive personas from scratch, and now they were convincing even one of the most powerful CEOs in the industry.

"Impressive," Ralph said after they finished their pitch. "I like I'm hearing. We should setup a meeting to discuss a couple of potential projects."

After Artie hung up, he immediately dialed another number. "Linda, darling! I've got some new friends who are just itching to make your acquaintance," Artie said, weaving a tale of Nate and Amy's remarkable achievements with the skill of a master storyteller. His voice resonated with sincerity and conviction, easily winning over the listener on the other end of the line.

As Artie made call after call, Nate marveled at his friend's persuasive abilities. He admired the ease with which Artie spun tales of their expertise, pulling strings and bending ears until even the most skeptical of individuals were clamoring to meet the dynamic duo.

"Seriously Artie, how do you do it?" Nate asked, taking a sip of the scotch Artie had poured for them.

"It's all about knowing the right people and telling the right stories," Artie said with a wry smile. "But you two are quite the package. It's been a long time since I've seen such natural chemistry and professionalism. We have a cocktail party to attend tonight," Artie announced "It's time for some face to face introductions with influential people."

Nate glanced at Amy, her red hair shimmering in the dim light like a fiery halo. She returned his gaze, her green eyes sparkling with determination.

***

The penthouse suite was a vision of opulence, from the sparkling crystal chandeliers to the gleaming marble floors. The city's elite were dressed in lavish gowns and tuxedos, their expensive jewelry glinting in the dim lighting.

Artie wasted no time, guiding them through the crowd with the confidence of a seasoned socialite.

"Ah, Ralph!" Artie exclaimed, approaching a silver-haired man with the air of a titan. "May I introduce Nathaniel and Amelia Everhart, the consultants I mentioned earlier?"

Artie's enthusiasm was contagious. He launched into another carefully crafted tale of their accomplishments, his voice dripping with admiration.

"Really?" Ralph asked, eyebrow raised in disbelief. "They managed to turn around that failing company in just three months?"

"Indeed," Artie replied, grinning broadly. "And they've got the skills and expertise to do the same for anyone smart enough to hire them."

As the evening wore on, Artie continued to introduce Nate and Amy to other influential individuals, each more skeptical than the last. But with each introduction, Artie's unwavering belief in their abilities and his skillful storytelling gradually won them over. Any initial doubts quickly faded from the eyes of their new acquaintances, Nate and Amy felt a huge surge of gratitude for their loyal friend.

"Artie, you're a miracle worker," Amy whispered to him as they left the party, the city lights twinkling below like a sea of diamonds.

"Ah, my dear," Artie replied, his eyes crinkling with amusement. "It's all smoke and mirrors. But remember, it's what you two do with these opportunities that truly matters."

Nate stood tall, his piercing blue eyes scanning the room as he sipped his champagne. His military background was evident in his posture, while Amy's investigative journalism background shone through her keen observation of the guests around them. The wealthy and powerful mingled at the opulent gala, their laughter and clinking glasses creating a symphony of indulgence.

"See that woman over there?" Artie whispered conspiratorially, nodding towards an impeccably dressed woman with silver hair and an air of authority. "That's Senator Diane Hawthorne. She's been looking for consultants to help her with her campaign strategy. This is your chance."

Nate exchanged a glance with Amy, who gave him a small nod. They approached the senator, Artie leading the way, his silver hair gleaming under the chandeliers.

"Senator Hawthorne," Artie beamed, extending his hand. "I'd like you to meet Nathaniel and Amelia Everhart, the brilliant minds behind some of the most successful campaigns in recent years."

Diane's gaze was cool and assessing, but she extended a well-manicured hand. "Arthur speaks highly of you," she remarked, her tone guarded.

"Artie has been very kind," Nate replied smoothly, his easy charm on full display. "But we believe our results truly speak for themselves."

"Results can be faked," Diane countered, her skepticism apparent.

"True," Amy chimed in, her eyes sparkling with intelligence. "But I doubt anyone could fabricate the complete overhaul of a corporate giant on the brink of collapse, all within a mere six months."

Diane raised an eyebrow, clearly intrigued. Sensing an opening, Artie launched into a captivating tale about how Nate and Amy had saved a multinational corporation from ruin, using their strategic thinking and innovative problem-solving skills.

"Very impressive," Diane admitted, her expression softening. "Perhaps we could discuss your ideas for my campaign further at a later date."

"Of course, Senator," Amy agreed, namedropping her contact information to the Senator's phone. "We'd be honored to help."

As the evening progressed, Nate and Amy were introduced to more skeptical influencers. But time and again, Artie artfully wielded his storytelling prowess, weaving a web of undeniable credibility around them.

When the gala finally wound down, Nate and Amy stepped out onto the balcony, the crisp night air invigorating their senses. They looked at each other, the weight of their accomplishment settling on their shoulders like an exquisite cloak.

"We did it, Nate," Amy breathed, her face alight with excitement. "We have the connections we need to move forward."

"Thanks to Artie's masterful storytelling," Nate added, his eyes gleaming with gratitude and determination. "Now, we can start making a difference."

The moonlit reflections on the gleaming high-rises mirrored the sparkle in Nate's eyes as he turned to Artie, extending a hand. "I can't thank you enough, Artie. Your loyalty and faith in us has made all the difference."

"Think nothing of it," Artie replied, taking Nate's hand with a firm grip. His silver hair glinted against the night sky, adding to his aura of sophistication. "You've always had my back, Nate. It's only fair that I return the favor."

Amy stepped forward, her striking red hair catching the city lights like fire. She hugged Artie, whispering in his ear, "You're family, Artie. We'll never forget what you've done for us."

As they released each other, Artie grinned, his eyes twinkling with mischief. "I must say, I haven't had this much fun spinning tales since we tried to sneak into the barracks after curfew during our military days!"

Nate chuckled at the memory, shaking his head. "We were lucky not to get caught then, but now, we have even more at stake."

"Indeed," Artie agreed, his expression turning serious. "But remember, I'm here for you both, every step of the way."

"Thank you, Artie," Nate said, his voice thick with emotion.

An electrifying charge of anticipation flowed through them all, as if the very air was charged with excitement. Nate and Amy exchanged glances, their expressions a mix of determination and exhilaration. With their cover story firmly established, they were poised to delve deeper into the shadows, righting wrongs and protecting the vulnerable.

"Alright then," Nate declared, clapping his hands together. "Let's get to work."

"Ready when you are," Amy added, her confidence contagious.

"Good luck, you two," Artie chimed in, his pride for his friends shining through. "I know you'll make a difference in this world."

As they turned to leave, Artie's words hung in the air like a promise. Nate and Amy knew that with their unbreakable partnership and Artie's unwavering support, the path ahead was theirs to forge. Bound by purpose and driven by justice, they stepped into the night, ready to put their cover story into action and take the first steps of an extraordinary journey.

And so, the next chapter of their mission began.

Chapter 4

Nate Everhart adjusted his cufflinks as he strode confidently into the luxurious restaurant, Amy on his arm. The sleek, tailored lines of their black attire made them look like they belonged amongst the rich and powerful who frequented this exclusive establishment. They exchanged a knowing glance, aware that tonight's performance had to be flawless.

The opulent setting of the restaurant enveloped them as they entered, a stark contrast to their actual lives. Crystal chandeliers cast a warm, intimate glow over the white linen-covered tables, each adorned with an intricate centerpiece of roses and orchids. The walls were covered in elaborate tapestries that told stories of a time long past, lending an air of sophistication to the atmosphere. Soft jazz emanated from hidden speakers, the sultry notes wrapping around them like a gentle embrace.

"Good evening," the impeccably dressed maître d' greeted them, offering a gracious smile that barely masked the calculating gleam in his eyes. "Do you have a reservation?"

"Of course," Nate replied smoothly, his voice deep and commanding. "Everhart, party of two."

"Ah, yes," the maître d' said, his eyes momentarily flickering to the computer screen before him. "Right this way, please." He led them through the maze of hushed conversations and clinking glasses, deftly avoiding the roaming waitstaff balancing trays of exquisite hors d'oeuvres.

As they walked, Amy's grip on his arm tightened ever so slightly. Her green eyes sparkled with anticipation, an investigative journalist background made her no stranger to high-pressure situations. They were a formidable team.

"Your table," the maître d' announced, gesturing towards an elegant booth nestled in a dimly lit corner of the restaurant. Nate could see the advantages of this location immediately - excellent visibility of the room while still remaining inconspicuous. "Enjoy your evening," the maître d' said, bowing his head slightly before disappearing back into the fray.

"Perfect," Nate murmured, his eyes scanning the room as they settled into their seats. Amy nodded in agreement, her gaze falling on a particularly ostentatious couple nearby. For a moment, she allowed herself a small, wry smile, knowing that beneath the opulence and grandeur of this world lay secrets, greed, and corruption - the very things they had set out to expose.

Nate leaned back in the plush chair, his fingers drumming on the table's polished surface. He was expecting to see an old acquaintance from his military days who now worked somewhat high up in Blackwood's organisation. Nate glanced casually around the restaurant and spotted the familiar face. He gave a subtle nod, and the man approached.

"Everhart, I didn't expect to see you here," the man said. His tailored suit and polished shoes revealed his newfound wealth, but there was still a hint of the soldier he once was. His posture. His hair, high and tight. Nate had tried growing his hair when he'd left the service as a way to "stick it to the man". It hadn't worked out too well, he hated having long hair. It wouldn't have been considered long to anyone outside of the military, but having hair touch his ears just wasn't something Nate could get used to.

"Ah, Jackson! Good to see you," Nate replied with a warm smile, his voice just loud enough to be overheard by nearby patrons.

They engaged in small talk before Jackson asked "So, what are you up to nowadays?" That was Nates opportunity. "Well, you'd never believe what I stumbled upon recently. An investment opportunity that's nothing short of groundbreaking."

Jackson raised an eyebrow, curiosity piqued. "Oh? Please don't start talking about crypto."

"Good God no", Nate continued, expertly walking the tightrope between mystery and revelation. "Imagine a technology, nothing to do with crypto, that could completely revolutionize a certain... highly profitable sector. I'm talking about returns that would make even the most jaded investor salivate."

While Nate engaged in conversation, Amy's eyes darted around the room, taking in the opulent dresses, glittering jewelry, and hushed conversations. She knew that tonight, her role was to observe, to look for any signs of Blackwood's arrival. Her keen senses were critical in spotting their target.

"Sounds intriguing," Jackson admitted, trying to suppress his interest. "But how do I know it's legit? You've always been one for... unconventional ventures."

"True," Nate conceded with a chuckle, knowing his past would lend credibility to the story. "But this time, it's different. This is a rare chance to be part of something truly extraordinary. And I trust you understand the value of discretion."

"Of course," Jackson said, his mind already racing with the possibilities. "I'll keep an ear to the ground."

"Much appreciated," Nate replied, clapping him on the back in a friendly manner as he returned to his seat.

Now that the seed was planted, it was only a matter of time before the information found its way to Blackwood. With a mixture of patience and anticipation, Nate turned his attention back to Amy, who was still scanning the room.

"Anything?" he asked, his voice low and urgent.

"Nothing yet," she replied, her eyes narrowing as she continued her search. "But I have a feeling he won't be far behind." There was a hint of humor in her tone, reminding Nate that, despite the gravity of their mission, they couldn't let it consume them entirely.

"Good," he murmured, his fingers drumming the table once more. "Let's make sure we're ready when he arrives."

Moments later, the restaurant's atmosphere shifted subtly, as if the air had become charged with an unseen current. Heads turned and conversations hushed, drawn to the imposing figure who had just entered the room. Sebastian Blackwood, flanked by his entourage of impeccably dressed associates, strode into the restaurant with the air of a king surveying his domain. It was a bit surreal, like something out of The Godfather. The cleaning business was obviously a front.

"Showtime," Nate murmured under his breath, exchanging a glance with Amy. Her eyes sparkled with determination. As Blackwood and his party made their way towards a private corner booth, Nate and Amy rose from their seats, their movements smooth and calculated.

"Excuse me," Nate said to a passing waiter, his tone dripping with false urgency. "My wife seems to have misplaced her earring. Could you kindly assist us in finding it?"

"Of course, sir," the waiter replied, his expression a mixture of concern and curiosity. He accompanied them to the area near Blackwood's table, where Nate and Amy began a convincing charade of searching for the nonexistent earring.

"Such a beautiful piece," Amy lamented, her voice loud enough to carry across the room. "A gift from my late father, you see. I would be devastated to lose it."

"Surely it must be here somewhere," Nate agreed, feigning frustration while surreptitiously keeping an eye on Blackwood. The businessman's attention flickered towards them, his brow furrowing as he attempted to place Nate's face. That was all they needed – a seed of recognition to take root.

"Ah! Here it is!" Amy exclaimed, holding up a small, glittering object in triumph. In reality, it was merely a spare earring she had brought along for this purpose. But it served its purpose, drawing the attention of Blackwood's entourage and cementing their presence in his mind.

"Thank you so much for your help," Nate said to the waiter, slipping a generous tip into his hand. "We truly appreciate it."

"Of course, sir," the waiter replied, pocketing the money with a grateful nod. As he departed, Nate and Amy settled themselves at their nearby table, affording them a clear view of Blackwood without appearing too conspicuous.

"Nicely done," Nate whispered, his eyes never leaving their target. Despite the gravity of the situation, he couldn't help but feel a thrill at the prospect of outwitting such a formidable adversary.

"Likewise," Amy replied, her voice steady and confident. "Now we just need to reel him in."

Nate smiled, his fingers drumming the table in anticipation. The game had begun, and they were playing for keeps.

Nate studied Blackwood from the corner of his eye, watching as the business tycoon sipped his wine and engaged in animated conversation with his entourage. His heart pounded in his chest, but he fought to maintain an outward appearance of calm as he signaled Amy with a slight nod.

"Here goes," he murmured under his breath, taking a sip of his own drink for courage.

As the waiter passed by their table, Nate caught his attention and leaned in, speaking in hushed tones. "This is subtle... but can you please make sure that Mr. Blackwood gets a taste of this exquisite wine? Tell him it's a gift from someone who appreciates his work."

"Of course, sir," the waiter replied, disappearing into the dimly lit room.

"Showtime," Amy whispered, her eyes sparkling with excitement and anticipation.

When the waiter presented the glass of wine to Blackwood, Nate seized the moment and locked eyes with the man, offering a discreet nod before returning his gaze to Amy. The message was clear: they were ready and willing to talk business.

It took only a few minutes for Blackwood to excuse himself from his entourage and approach their table, his curiosity piqued by the leaked information from Jackson and Nate's confident demeanor.

"Mr. Everhart, I presume?" he said, extending a hand to Nate. "Sebastian Blackwood. I must say, I'm quite intrigued by what I've heard about your little... venture."

"Mr. Blackwood," Nate replied, shaking his hand firmly. "It's an honor to meet you in person. And yes, our venture has certainly been generating some buzz. Allow me to introduce my wife and partner, Amy."

"Charmed," Blackwood said, inclining his head towards Amy, who offered a polite smile in return.

"Thank you for joining us, Sebastian," Nate continued, gesturing towards an empty chair. "We believe this opportunity is too good not to share with someone as influential and respected as yourself."

"Indeed," Blackwood mused, taking a seat and swirling the wine in his glass. "I must admit, I am eager to learn more."

Nate could hardly contain his excitement as he shared a knowing glance with Amy. The bait had been taken; now it was time to reel

CHECKMATE

him in. As Nate began speaking in earnest about the groundbreaking technology or investment opportunity they were offering, he knew with every fiber of his being that they had set the stage for something truly momentous.

"Sebastian," Nate said, leaning forward and lowering his voice, "we'd be honored if you would attend a private meeting to discuss this further, where we can provide you with all the information you need to make an informed decision."

"Very well," Blackwood agreed, a calculating glint in his eyes. "I look forward to it."

Nate leaned in, his voice low and conspiratorial. "Allow me to share a glimpse of the brilliance at your fingertips. Picture this: AI-driven software that not only predicts market trends but also adapts and learns from its own predictions, creating an ever-evolving tool for unprecedented financial success."

Blackwood's eyes widened, the flicker of greed igniting within them. Amy could see the wheels turning in his mind - the allure of power, wealth, and influence even greater than what he already possessed.

"Interesting," Blackwood said, his tone measured. "But surely, such technology must have its limitations."

"Ah, but that's where you're mistaken," Nate replied, a grin tugging at the corner of his mouth. "This AI is like no other. Its adaptive learning capabilities outpace anything currently on the market."

Amy chimed in, her voice smooth and confident. "Not to mention the proprietary algorithms we've developed to ensure the software remains at the cutting edge of the industry. We've spent years perfecting it, refining our techniques and strategies."

"Years?" Blackwood raised an eyebrow, clearly impressed by their dedication.

"Absolutely," Amy confirmed, her green eyes locked onto his. "We believe in the potential of this technology, and we know that it has the capacity to revolutionize the way business is conducted globally."

"Consider the possibilities, Sebastian," Nate urged. "A world where you can predict market fluctuations with uncanny accuracy – where fortunes are made at the whim of a few lines of code. The opportunities are limitless, and they're all within reach."

Blackwood's gaze darted between Nate and Amy, the air around him charged with anticipation. As he contemplated their words, Amy caught Nate's eye, giving him a subtle nod. It was time to drive the point home.

"Tell me," Blackwood finally spoke, his voice slow and deliberate, "how do I know I can trust you?"

"A valid concern," Nate conceded, nodding sagely. "Allow me to assuage your fears."

As Nate began to regale Blackwood with tales of their past successes and accolades, Amy took the opportunity to study their mark. The man was a master of hiding his emotions, a formidable poker player, but she could sense the hunger gnawing at him – the relentless drive for more.

"Sebastian," she interjected, her tone gentle yet firm, "we understand that trust is earned, not given. That's why we're here tonight, to prove ourselves to you. If our words aren't enough, let our actions speak for themselves."

"Indeed," Nate agreed, his eyes never leaving Blackwood's face. "We are confident in our expertise, our knowledge, and our ability to deliver on our promises."

Their words hung in the air like a delicate dance of persuasion, each syllable expertly crafted to captivate and enthrall. And as Amy watched the play of emotions across Blackwood's features, she knew without a doubt that they had succeeded in ensnaring him – hook, line, and sinker.

Nate leaned back in his chair, a wicked glint in his eyes as he allowed the silence to stretch between them. The soft tinkling of piano keys accompanied the hushed murmurs of fellow diners, creating an atmosphere of subdued elegance within the dimly lit restaurant. Nate could tell that Blackwood was on the precipice of biting the bait, and all that was needed was one final nudge.

"Sebastian," he began, his voice low and conspiratorial, "I can see that you are intrigued by what we've discussed so far. However, I believe that our true potential can only be realized through a more in-depth conversation."

Amy watched with carefully veiled pride as Nate artfully navigated the delicate balance between piquing their target's interest and maintaining an air of exclusivity. She knew that her husband's natural charisma and intelligence made him the perfect partner for this dance of persuasion, and she eagerly awaited his next move.

Blackwood's icy blue eyes narrowed at Nate's words, but there was no mistaking the spark of curiosity that flickered within them. He glanced around the room, taking note of the wealthy patrons who were now surreptitiously observing their exchange – no doubt wondering what these three individuals could possibly have to discuss that warranted such secrecy.

"Very well," he acquiesced, his tone guarded yet intrigued. "When and where do you propose this meeting take place?"

Nate ran a hand through his dark hair. "Always straight to business, aren't you? Well, how about two days from now? We can arrange a location that ensures both privacy and security – after all, we wouldn't want any unwanted ears listening in on our conversation, would we?"

Blackwood mulled over the offer, weighing his options and calculating the potential gains. Amy caught a glimpse of something akin to greed flickering in his eyes, and she knew that they had successfully appealed to his ambitions.

"Very well," Blackwood agreed, a thin smile gracing his features. "Two days it is. I'll have my assistant contact you with the details. And let me be clear – I expect complete discretion from both of you."

"Of course," Nate replied smoothly, raising his glass in a toast as Amy mirrored the gesture. "To new beginnings and prosperous partnerships."

The glasses clinked together, their crystalline notes echoing throughout the room like a siren's song – the chorus of a dance that was far from over. As they drank to their upcoming meeting, Nate and Amy shared a secret smile, knowing full well the next phase of their plan was about to begin.

"Two days it is," Blackwood confirmed, gently tapping the table with his well-manicured fingers. "I'll be looking forward to it."

"Likewise," Nate replied, a subtle tension in his jaw betraying the effort it took to maintain his composed facade.

"Until then," Amy added, her voice a honeyed lullaby that seemed to wrap around the entire room.

With polite nods and firm handshakes, the trio exchanged final pleasantries before parting ways. The moment Blackwood turned his back, Nate's gaze locked onto Amy's, an unspoken understanding passing between them as they began their strategic exit from the restaurant.

Their steps were measured and unhurried, each footfall echoing softly against the polished marble floor. The low hum of conversation buzzed around them, punctuated by the occasional tinkle of laughter or clink of glassware. All the while, they remained on high alert, acutely aware of the need for discretion.

"Phase one complete," Nate mused inwardly, allowing himself a small, self-congratulatory smile. His thoughts drifted momentarily to the private meeting they had successfully arranged – a crucial step towards achieving their ultimate goal.

Amy nodded silently, her eyes scanning the room one last time as they neared the exit. Her attention to detail had been critical earlier, and now she was ensuring their escape went unnoticed.

"Never a dull moment, huh?" Nate thought, the corners of his mouth lifting into a smirk as they slipped past a group of patrons engaged in animated conversation. Their departure went wholly unobserved, just as they had planned.

"Wouldn't have it any other way," Amy conceded with a mental chuckle, her hand resting lightly on the small of Nate's back as they stepped into the dimly lit foyer.

"Careful, darling," he warned her playfully. "We wouldn't want anyone to think we're actually enjoying ourselves."

"Perish the thought," she retorted, her voice a conspiratorial whisper as they shared a brief, knowing glance.

With one last look over their shoulders, Nate and Amy stepped out into the night, leaving behind the opulent confines of the restaurant and its unsuspecting patrons. As they made their way down the moonlit street, their minds were already racing ahead, meticulously mapping out the next phase of their plan – a delicate dance between deception and desire that would push them to the limits of their cunning and skill.

"Ready for the next move?" Amy asked softly, her breath fogging in the chilly air.

"Always," Nate replied, his eyes gleaming with anticipation as they vanished into the shadows, preparing for the intricate game that lay ahead.

***

Back inside the restaurant, Sebastian Blackwood leaned back in his plush velvet chair, swirling the remnants of his expensive wine in its glass. The dimly lit room cast shadows across his chiseled features as he mulled over the intriguing conversation he had just shared with Nate and Amy.

"Mr. Blackwood," one of his entourage members, a young man with slicked-back hair and an audacious tie, ventured cautiously, "is everything alright?"

"Better than alright, Thomas," Blackwood replied, his voice low and smooth as silk. "I think I've just stumbled upon something... quite remarkable."

"Sir?" another associate, a woman with a no-nonsense bob and impeccably tailored suit, inquired, her eyebrows raised in intrigue.

"An opportunity," Blackwood revealed, his eyes gleaming in the candlelight. "One that could change the game entirely. It's been a long time since I've felt this... excited."

"Sounds promising," the woman remarked, masking her surprise at Blackwood's uncharacteristic show of emotion. "What's the plan?"

"First, we arrange a private meeting," Blackwood said, tapping his fingers on the polished wooden table. "Somewhere discreet. Somewhere secure."

"Of course," the woman nodded, making a mental note to begin preparations as soon as possible.

"Then, we'll see if this 'groundbreaking technology' is all it's cracked up to be," Blackwood continued, a hint of skepticism creeping into his tone. "If it is, well... let's just say the world will never be the same again."

"Quite the bold claim, sir," Thomas interjected, trying to keep up with the conversation. "But if anyone can pull it off, it's you."

"Flattery will get you nowhere, Thomas," Blackwood chided, though the corners of his lips betrayed the faintest hint of a smile. "But you're not wrong. If this opportunity lives up to its potential, it will cement my legacy as one of the most influential men in history."

"High stakes," the woman mused, her gaze flicking to where Nate and Amy had just been sitting moments before. "Do you trust them?"

"Trust?" Blackwood scoffed, swirling his wine again. "Trust is for fools, my dear. But I do believe they have something of value. And I intend to find out exactly what that is."

"Then we'll be ready for whatever comes next," she said firmly, her eyes meeting Blackwood's with steely resolve.

"Indeed," Blackwood agreed, finishing the last of his wine before setting down the glass with a decisive clink. "Let the games begin."

As the final echoes of his words dissipated into the hushed conversations of the restaurant, a palpable sense of anticipation settled over their small corner of the room. With the wheels now set in motion, Sebastian Blackwood and his entourage prepared themselves for the high-stakes dance that awaited them, each harboring their own thoughts and motivations as they gazed into the unknown.

And so, the stage was set for the thrilling next chapter in this intricate game of deception and desire.

Chapter 5

The city lights danced like a sea of fireflies against the encroaching dusk as the elevator doors parted with a hushed whisper. Nathaniel "Nate" Everhart, his silhouette sharpened by the tailored cut of his charcoal suit, stepped into the penthouse suite that loomed high above the urban sprawl. Amelia "Amy" Everhart followed, her red hair a flame against the neutral palette of their clandestine meeting place.

"Sebastian Blackwood," Nate boomed, his voice rich with the timbre of confidence, his hand extended in an offer of warmth that belied the chill in his heart.

Blackwood rose from a leather chair, the skyline framing him like a titan among men. "Nathaniel," he greeted, his handshake firm, the steel in his eyes betraying nothing of the scrutiny he subjected them to.

Amy's gaze swept the room discreetly, noting the opulence that spoke of Blackwood's successes—successes built on the backs of others. Her mind ticked over each detail, storing it away for later use. She remained silent, a sentinel amid the pleasantries exchanged.

"Quite the view you've got here, Bastian," Nate said, stepping towards the floor-to-ceiling windows, the city spread out beneath them—a chessboard waiting for its kings and pawns to play out this game of wits.

"Only the best, for the best," Blackwood replied, a smirk playing at the corner of his lips. The words hung between them, a veiled challenge that Nate was all too eager to accept.

"Indeed," Nate murmured, turning back to face Blackwood. He observed the man before him, the once-bully turned charmer. Nate knew how to play this game; he had mastered it in the shadows of military strategy and the quiet hum of computer servers.

"Let's get down to business, shall we?" Blackwood suggested, motioning to the mahogany table that bore witness to countless deals and shattered dreams.

"Of course," Nate said, the words clipped, his smile never reaching his eyes. He took the seat opposite Blackwood, the table a chasm of unspoken truths between them.

Amy slid into the chair beside Nate, her expression composed, her mind a whirlwind. She read the room, the tension, the stakes—they were familiar companions in her quest for justice, for those wronged like her father had been.

"Your reputation precedes you," Nate began, leaning in, his voice a tool that wielded charm as deftly as a scalpel. "A self-made man, an empire at your fingertips."

"Flattery will get you everywhere, Mr. Everhart," Blackwood quipped, though the glint of interest in his eye betrayed his pleasure at the recognition.

"Then let's hope it takes us right to where we need to be," Nate countered, his grin wolfish. His fingers tapped a staccato rhythm on the tabletop, betraying none of the adrenaline coursing through his veins.

Amy, her eyes sharp, watched the interplay, ready to pounce, to steer, to conquer. The dance had begun, and she was poised to take the lead when the moment called for it.

The city below seemed to hold its breath, awaiting the outcome of this high-stakes performance. Nate and Amy were players on a stage set for deception, but with each calculated move, they drew the curtain back on corruption. And as the night deepened, so did their resolve.

Above them, the chandelier dripped crystals like icicles over a winter market, casting prismatic shadows across Blackwood's lined face. He sat, fortress-like, behind a mahogany desk that could have doubled as a Viking banquet table.

"Mr. Blackwood," Nate said, his voice threading through the opulence with the ease of a well-played note, "your ventures in the real estate market were nothing short of visionary."

Blackwood's chest puffed slightly, the corners of his mouth twitching upwards. "Vision is merely the first step," he responded, leaning back into the embrace of his leather chair.

"Indeed," Nate nodded, catching Amy's subtle cue from the corner of his eye. She shifted imperceptibly, her red hair a flame against the cool backdrop of city lights.

"And vision," Amy interjected smoothly, her tone both deferential and assured, "is what sets apart the pioneers in artificial intelligence—particularly in the stock market forecasts. The potential for growth there is exponential."

Blackwood's interest visibly sharpened, like the edge of a blade glinting in moonlight. "Go on," he urged, steepling his fingers.

"Imagine," she continued, her words painting the future with each syllable, "an AI that can sift through global financial data in microseconds, predicting trends, guiding investments..."

"Like a modern oracle," Blackwood mused, his eyes reflecting not just the skyline but the shine of unmined coins.

"Exactly," Amy concurred, her red hair a silent siren in the room's controlled ambiance. "And your esteemed aptitude for seizing opportunity could be...revolutionized."

Nate watched as the seeds of greed took root in Blackwood's imagination, his military-honed instincts gauging the tycoon's response, measuring the pull of the bait.

"Revolutionized," Blackwood repeated, tasting the word, rolling it around his tongue like a vintage wine. "I do like the sound of that."

Nate leaned forward, the city's neon veins pulsing through the penthouse windows, casting a predator's gleam in his eyes. "Let's talk specifics," he said, each word a calculated step on the chessboard of persuasion.

"Angel investing," Amy chimed in, her voice a velvet hammer, "is about foresight and influence. You're not just betting on horses, Bastian—you're sculpting the race."

Blackwood's gaze flickered between them, interest piqued. "The numbers," he demanded, fingers tapping an impatient rhythm on the armrest.

"We're looking at a twenty percent stake," Nate stated. "A gateway to uncharted profits." He slid a sleek tablet across the table, graphs and figures waltzing across the screen with a tap of his finger. "Picture it—your capital shaping market frontiers."

Amy watched Blackwood absorb the data, her mind tracing their plan's next move. His greed was palpable, a scent they could almost taste.

She texted "Now" and pressed send.

"Status," Nate pressed on, "the kind that opens every door, whispers your name in every high-stakes circle. That's the real currency here."

"Exponential growth..." Amy's observation hung in the air like an invitation, "...in both wealth and prestige."

"Indeed?" Blackwood leaned in, the hook sinking deeper.

Before another word could be exchanged, the door opened with a silent assertion of wealth. Chloe Grant stepped into the room, the embodiment of success in her tailored dress, every seam whispering exclusivity. She held the attention as if it were on a diamond-studded leash.

"Sebastian Blackwood, meet Chloe Grant," Nate introduced, a knowing smile playing on his lips. "A testament to the very opportunity we're discussing."

"Mr. Blackwood." Chloe's voice was a melody of confidence, her handshake firm, the contact brief yet impactful. "I've seen firsthand what foresight in AI investments can yield. It's not just impressive—it's transformative."

Blackwood, ever the shark, eyed Chloe with newfound calculation. The presence of tangible success reshaped the contours of possibility in his mind. Nate felt the momentum shift, the threads of their plan weaving tighter around their mark.

"Transformative," Blackwood echoed, his voice a low hum of intrigue. "You have my attention."

Nate and Amy exchanged a glance, the electric current of their strategy crackling unseen. They were in. Now to reel him in, to bind him to their cause until the trap was set and escape was but a dream in the business tycoon's ambitious heart.

Chloe perched on the arm of a leather chair, the city lights glinting off her wristwatch, a beacon of her success. Her eyes locked onto Blackwood's, a challenge and promise rolled into one.

"Imagine," she began, her voice smooth as top-shelf whiskey, "tripling your net worth in much less than a fiscal year. That was my reality after betting on the right horse—artificial intelligence."

Blackwood leaned forward, his gaze sharpening, assessing. The air in the penthouse seemed charged with the scent of money and ambition.

"Tripling?" Blackwood asked, skepticism lacing his tone, but his posture betrayed his interest.

"Absolutely," Chloe confirmed, with a nod so subtle it was almost imperceptible. "And I'm not just talking figures on a screen. It's the doors that open—the ones you didn't even know existed."

Nate watched from the sidelines, his fingers tapping an invisible code on his thigh. He could read the hunger in Blackwood's eyes, the same look he'd seen in countless others before they took the bait.

Amy pressed send on a second text.

"Opportunity is a fleeting guest, Mr. Blackwood." Chloe stood, smoothing her dress as if brushing away any doubt. "It knocks softly and leaves swiftly. You wouldn't want to regret missing it."

Before Blackwood could craft a reply, the door swung open again, this time revealing a man whose casual demeanor clashed with the previous entrance. Miles sauntered in wearing a grin and a blazer that hung off his shoulders as if stitched from the very notion of leisure.

"Sebastian, allow me to introduce Miles Thompson," Nate said, gesturing to the newcomer. "He's living proof that our venture goes beyond mere profits; it's about lifestyle."

Miles offered a handshake, his grip easy yet firm, a balance between camaraderie and confidence. "You know, I was skeptical too, Bastian. But here I am, less tied down to the office, more time for the finer things."

Nate observed Blackwood's reaction closely, the slight tilt of his head, the narrowed eyes scanning Miles as if trying to find the catch in the pitch. It was all part of the dance, and Nate knew the steps by heart.

"More time?" Blackwood repeated, the words rolling off his tongue, flavored with intrigue.

"Sure," Miles replied, thumbing the lapel of his jacket. "The AI does the heavy lifting, crunches the numbers while I enjoy life."

Inside Nate's chest, his heart kept a steady beat, a silent drum heralding their advancement. This was it—the push and pull, the careful orchestration of desire and fear, the human psyche laid bare and malleable. And they were sculpting it to their design.

"Interesting," Blackwood murmured, his fingers steepled, his mind undoubtedly racing through scenarios of wealth and leisure.

Nate could almost hear the gears turning, could sense the shift as greed edged out caution. They had him leaning in, now to tip the scales.

"Time is precious, Sebastian," Nate chimed in, his voice a velvet hammer. "We're merely offering you a way to buy more of it."

In the silence that followed, laden with thoughts of what could be, Nate knew they had scored a direct hit on Blackwood's aspirations. Now to wait, to let the seed of possibility germinate into a decision they all wanted.

Miles leaned back in his chair, the leather creaking under his casual sprawl. He fixed Blackwood with a congenial smile that held the soft glint of gold—a promise. "Let me tell you, Sebastian," he began, the air around him charged with the heat of whispered secrets, "when I first heard about this AI system, I was skep—"

"Of course, you were," Blackwood interjected, mirroring Miles's posture. The tycoon's skepticism hung palpably in the room, a thin veil of smoke.

"—tical," Miles continued, undeterred. "But then I saw my first quarter's returns." His hand mimicked an airplane taking off, and the room followed its trajectory. "Sky-high profits, my friend."

Nate, standing by the window, watched as Blackwood's eyes flicked to Amy, searching her face for confirmation. Amy, ever the astute observer, caught the glance and nodded subtly. Her red hair framed her face like a halo of credibility.

"That was just in the early stages. We've tweaked and improved the system since. Exclusive access, Sebastian," she chimed in, her voice cutting through the tension with surgical precision. "High risk, yes, but even higher reward."

"Ah, exclusivity," Blackwood mused, tapping a finger against the polished surface of the table. "A commodity in itself these days."

"Indeed," Nate said, his voice steady as he walked over and perched on the arm of a sofa, close enough to be conspiratorial. "We're not casting a wide net here. It's a select few who will ride this wave."

"Exactly," Chloe added, her statement punctuated by the clink of ice in her glass. "The kind of opportunity that doesn't knock twice."

Blackwood's gaze swept from Miles to Chloe, then rested on Nate. "You understand it takes more than fancy numbers to impress me," he said, his tone probing.

"Of course," Nate replied, his mind racing like a seasoned hacker through firewalls of doubt. "It's not just the profit—it's the edge it gives you. In your world, information is power, and this... this is the ultimate insider tip."

"Without the legal hassle," Amy interjected smoothly, her words painting a picture of a world free from consequence, a siren call to a man like Blackwood.

"Imagine having the foresight to anticipate market shifts before anyone else," Miles said, leaning forward, elbows on knees, ensnaring Blackwood with a shared vision of the future.

"Imagine the influence," Amy whispered, as if confiding a sacred truth. Her words hung in the air, heavy with implication.

"Enough to outmaneuver any competitor," Nate concluded, sealing the pact with finality.

And there it was—the hook, the line, and the sinker. The game of chess played out in veiled words and sharpened glances. Blackwood's cold exterior thawed, a crack in the ice revealing the current beneath.

"Tell me more," he said, and Nate could sense the shift in balance, the careful tipping of scales. The plan was unfolding, each move calculated, each player essential. And the endgame was near, a checkmate dressed as an invitation to an elite club where entry was not just bought, but earned.

Nate leaned back, his fingers steepled as he regarded Sebastian Blackwood with a discerning eye. The dying light of the day filtered through the expansive windows of the penthouse suite, casting long shadows that stretched across the polished floor like tendrils reaching for the tycoon.

"Sebastian," Nate said, the timbre of his voice low and compelling, "I trust you see the value we've laid out before you. However, this venture waits for no one."

Amy stood by the window, her silhouette framed against the sprawling cityscape. She turned slightly, the red in her hair flaring like embers as she caught the last ray of sunlight. Her eyes locked with Blackwood's, sharp and calculating.

"Time is the currency of opportunity," she voiced crisply. "And right now, it's trading at a premium."

Blackwood's brow furrowed, the gears in his mind visibly turning. He shifted in his chair; the leather creaked beneath him—a sound like caution giving way to desire.

"Indeed," he murmured, his gaze flitting between the two masterminds and their living success stories. "What's the deadline?"

"Midnight, tomorrow," Nate said, dropping the words like a guillotine's blade. "It's exclusive, Bastian. For visionaries only."

The urgency rippled through the room, a tangible force that seemed to quicken the pulse of the conversation. Amy took a step forward, her heels clicking against the marble like a metronome set to the tempo of opportunity.

"Think of it," she coaxed, "as your personal renaissance. A pivot point where history remembers your name."

Chloe, ever the embodiment of poise, nodded in agreement, her diamond earrings catching the light and scattering it across the room like stardust. Miles, with his effortless charm, lounged against an opulent armchair, his smile an echo of victories past and those yet to be claimed.

Blackwood rose from his seat, towering over the ensemble. His shadow loomed large, but his eyes held a new glint—excitement edged with the raw hunger of ambition.

"Extraordinary," he said, running a hand through his greying hair. "That's how I built my empire. By being part of something extraordinary."

"Exactly," Nate affirmed, standing to meet Blackwood's posture inch for inch. "You didn't get where you are by hesitating at the gates of greatness."

"Nor will I start now," Blackwood declared, extending his hand. "Tell me what I need to do."

Nate clasped Blackwood's hand firmly, the deal etching itself into the twilight of the room. Amy's lips curved into a faint, almost imperceptible smile. The pieces were moving; the board was set.

"Welcome to the future," Nate said, releasing Blackwood's hand. "We'll send everything over tonight."

"Looking forward to it," Blackwood replied, the anticipation in his voice a low thrum, barely contained.

As Blackwood escorted them to the door, Nate could feel the weight of their exit—a departure heavy with the promise of things to come. The air was charged, crackling with the electricity of a storm on the horizon. They were in. Now came the real work.

***

The penthouse door clicked shut behind them, sealing the deal within its opulent walls. Nate straightened his tie with a quick flick of his wrist, a small but telling action that spoke volumes to Amy. They began their descent, the plush carpet of the corridor hushing their steps as they moved in tandem toward the elevator.

"Think he bought it?" Amy's voice was low, tinged with the thrill of the hunt.

"Hook, line, and sinker," Nate replied, a wolfish grin briefly breaking his composed facade. His eyes were alive, alight with the fire of a man who'd just set the stage for an act of grand retribution.

The elevator dinged, its doors sliding open with silent efficiency. They stepped inside, enveloped by the reflective chrome interior that cast their images back at them—a pair of avenging angels cloaked in bespoke attire. As the doors closed, Amy leaned against the mirrored wall, her red hair a stark contrast to the sterile shine.

"Chloe and Miles played their parts well," she mused, watching Nate's reflection as he nodded.

"Couldn't have done it without them," he agreed, pressing the ground floor button with more force than necessary. "But Blackwood's ego... that's our best ally."

As the elevator descended, Nate's thoughts raced through the intricacies of their plan. Each step was a calculated move on a chessboard of their own design, and Blackwood was their unwitting king, maneuvered into position for a checkmate he never saw coming.

"Risks?" Amy probed, her green eyes locking onto Nate's in the mirror.

"Plenty," he admitted, the weight of their endeavor pressing down like the gravity of the descending lift. "He's not one to take lightly. We're playing on his turf."

"Then we'd better be damn good at the game." A corner of Amy's mouth quirked up, her confidence as infectious as it was necessary.

CHECKMATE

"Always are," Nate countered, his exterior calm belying the adrenaline coursing through him. He'd been in tougher spots—in the military, every decision could mean life or death. This was different, yet familiar; another kind of battlefield where the enemy wore suits and wielded power instead of guns.

When the doors opened, they stepped out into the lobby, the click of Amy's heels punctuating the stillness like the ticking of a clock counting down to an inevitable endgame. They crossed the polished marble floor, approaching the glass entrance that led out into the night.

"Ready for what's next?" Nate asked as they pushed through the doors, the cool evening air brushing against their faces.

Amy matched his stride, determination etched in her every step. "Let's bring down an empire," she said, her voice as steady as her resolve.

Nate glanced sidelong at her, admiration mingling with affection. Together, they strode into the darkness, the city lights reflecting off the building façades around them—silent witnesses to the unfolding drama. The echo of their footsteps faded into the hum of the city, two shadows merging with the night, their mission far from over.

"Empires don't crumble in a day," Nate murmured.

"Then we chip away, night after night," Amy replied, her tone edged with the steel of unyielding resolve.

The click-clack of their steps was a staccato rhythm against the concrete as they made their way down the dimly lit street. The occasional siren wail pierced the night, a reminder of the chaos that lurked beneath the surface.

Nate's mind raced, each thought a bullet train barreling through the possibilities and pitfalls that lay ahead. They had Blackwood's ear, but trust was a currency that could flip its value in an instant. Every word spoken, every glance exchanged, had to be calculated with precision—there was no room for error.

He felt Amy's hand brush against his, a silent message of solidarity. Their alliance was more than mere partnership; it was the fusion of two forces, both scarred by past injustices, both hungry for retribution.

"Chloe and Miles played their parts well," he said, glancing at her profile bathed in the neon glow of a passing sign. "But Blackwood's no fool. He'll test the waters before diving in."

"Which is why we'll be ready with every answer," she shot back, a smirk gracing her lips. "We've laid the groundwork. Now comes the finesse."

They reached the car, a nondescript sedan that blended with the night. Nate unlocked the door, and the familiar scent of leather greeted them—an olfactory cue to shift gears, to move from persuasion to action.

"Artie's intel says Blackwood's got another deal brewing—something big," Nate said as he slid into the driver's seat, the engine purring to life under his touch.

"Let him play his hand. We'll be there to call his bluff," Amy said, fastening her seatbelt with a decisive click.

As they pulled away from the curb, the rearview mirror captured a last glimpse of the penthouse suite, now just another box of light amongst countless others. It stood as a beacon of false security, a castle built on sand.

Their path was fraught with dangers, a labyrinthine plot that would require all their cunning to navigate. But as the city swallowed them whole, there was an electric charge in the air—the spark of an upcoming storm. With each mile they put behind them, the promise of justice, of exposing the rot at the core of Blackwood's empire, drew nearer.

"Next stop, the belly of the beast," Nate said, his voice steady despite the adrenaline that coursed through him.

"Then let's not keep the beast waiting," Amy returned, her eyes alight with the thrill of the hunt.

Chapter 6

Sebastian Blackwood's eyes flickered with a predatory gleam, the kind that came from sniffing out the scent of money. He stood in his office, a panorama of the city sprawling beneath him like a chessboard waiting for his next master stroke. His fingers danced over the sleek surface of his mahogany desk, a rhythmic tap-tap-tapping that matched the quickening pulse of his excitement—this investment was ballooning, and he was tethered to its ascent.

"Everhart," he mumbled to himself, his voice a low rumble, "you've got quite the little gold mine here."

The venture had started as a mere blip on his financial radar, but now it threatened to outshine his other endeavors, pulling him into its orbit with the promise of unprecedented returns. It wasn't just about the money anymore; it was the thrill, the game, the conquest.

***

CHECKMATE

"Blackwood's hooked, Amy," Nate said, scrolling through the latest reports on his laptop. His finger paused over the touchpad. "Time to reel him in." The corners of his mouth twitched upward, the closest thing to a smile when he was on the hunt.

"Set the stage?" Amy asked, her red hair catching the light as she leaned over his shoulder, peering at the screen.

"His office. Tomorrow. We'll lay out the numbers, dazzle him with potential." Nate's voice carried the certainty of a man who knew how to play this game—no, orchestrate it. They were going to not only show Blackwood the carrot but make him believe it was his idea to chase it.

"Got it." Amy's fingers flew over her phone, setting things in motion. She was a maestro of logistics, each detail finessed with precision. "I'll arrange the meeting."

Nate watched her work, admiration lacing through the pride he felt. They were an unbreakable unit, two sides of the same coin, forged through trials and cemented in trust.

"Remember, we're offering him the future," Nate said, closing his laptop with a decisive click. "A future where he thinks he wins."

Amy grinned, a flash of shared conspiracy. "But we write the ending."

"Always," Nate replied, standing up. His past—a blend of military discipline and hacking mischief—had taught him one thing: the line between right and wrong was often blurred, but their mission was clear. Exploiters like Blackwood would never see them coming until it was too late.

"Let's go prep," Amy said, tucking her phone away. "We've got a tycoon to impress—and a snake to defang."

With a nod, they moved together toward their makeshift war room. Sebastian Blackwood might have been a giant in his world, but Nate and Amy Everhart were about to remind him that even giants could fall.

The conference room was a battleground of opulence, every inch designed to intimidate. Heavy mahogany doors swung open, ushering Nate and Amy into the lair where Sebastian Blackwood reigned. His empire sprawled around him in panoramic views of the city, a testament to his ironclad grip on power.

"Sebastian," Nate began, his voice smooth as he slid a glossy brochure across the table. "You've seen the numbers. The returns are impressive, but they're just the beginning."

Blackwood, perched like an eagle at the head of the table, arched a silvered eyebrow. "Go on," he rumbled cautiously.

Amy leaned forward, red hair framing her face like flames. "We're talking about exponential growth. But to achieve that, we need to scale up. Consider doubling your investment."

A flicker of doubt crossed Blackwood's features. He steepled his fingers, eyes narrowing. "They're good", he thought, "playing me with bait for greed". Nate's gaze held no guile, Amy's enthusiasm seemed sincere. Yet, a whisper of wariness wound through Blackwood's mind. More money, more risk.

"Exponential is a seductive word," Blackwood said slowly, the timber of his voice betraying a hint of skepticism. "But one doesn't amass wealth by being seduced."

"True," Amy countered, her tone matching his stride for stride. "But you also don't amass it by playing safe. We're not asking you to gamble; we're presenting an opportunity to own the game."

Blackwood's thoughts raced behind a stoic facade. An opportunity or a trap? The shadows of past dealings flickered in his memory—times when charm had yielded more than brute force ever could. He wasn't unaccustomed to high stakes, but this was different. Could this be my crowning glory, or are these two setting me up for a fall?

Nate observed the titan before them, noting the minute clench of jaw, the almost imperceptible tightening around the eyes. "Sebastian, imagine the legacy you could build. This isn't just about wealth; it's about reshaping the industry. You have the vision for it—we're simply providing the tools."

Blackwood mulled over their words, the enticing promise of legacy wrestling with the primal instinct of self-preservation. He gazed out at the cityscape, his city, weighing the scales of ambition against the guttural tug of caution.

"Legacy," he echoed, the word hanging between them like a challenge. He turned back, eyes locking with Nate's. "I'll need more details. Concrete evidence that this isn't just smoke and mirrors."

"Understandable," Amy said with a nod, ready with folders full of charts and projections. "Let's dive into the specifics then, shall we?"

Nate watched Blackwood's demeanor, gauging each nuanced shift in posture, every probing question. They were threading the needle between arousing his appetite for success and not triggering his alarm bells.

The air crackled with the tension of a high-stakes poker game, each player keenly aware that the next move could alter the course of the match. And while Blackwood weighed his empire against the glittering lure of a future even grander, Nate and Amy waited, the architects of persuasion, poised to construct their most audacious illusion yet.

The clock on the wall ticked with a resonance that felt like the heartbeat of the city itself, each second reverberating through the spacious office where fortunes were made and lost. Sebastian Blackwood sat, his fingers steepled, eyes narrowed in contemplation as he considered the glossy brochures spread before him.

"Time is of the essence, Bastian," Nate said, leaning forward, the evening light casting his face in half-shadow, adding an air of mystery to his already compelling presence. "We're talking about a limited window here. The terms are exclusive—reserved for visionaries who act swiftly."

Amy's eyes sparkled as she interjected, her voice smooth and convincing. "And the perks, well, they're not just financial. This will provide greater access. Connections. People you've wanted on your speed dial for years."

Blackwood's gaze flickered between them, the bait dangling tantalizingly close. He could almost taste the rarefied air of the upper echelons that seemed one bold move away.

"Connections?" he repeated, interest piqued. His mind churned, envisioning the doors that might open, the hands he'd shake, the silent nods of recognition across crowded rooms.

"Absolutely," Amy affirmed, standing to pace, the movement drawing Blackwood's attention. Her heels clicked decisively on the hardwood floor, a metronome of urgency. "But these opportunities? They evaporate. You know how it works—the early bird doesn't just get the worm; he gets the juiciest, fattest ones."

Nate watched the tycoon, noting the flare of desire in Blackwood's eyes, then the quick, guarded shutter. He knew Blackwood was a man who'd built empires by seizing moments just like this one.

"Think of it, Bastian," Nate pressed, tapping the brochure for emphasis. "Others are already climbing aboard. People you respect. They see the potential."

"Who?" Blackwood demanded, leaning in despite himself, the scent of opportunity overpowering the musty odor of hesitation.

"Names you'd know. Movers. Shakers." Nate's words were deliberate, each one stoking the fire of Blackwood's ambition while caressing his ego.

"Can't reveal names without higher investment, confidentiality clauses," Amy added, her fingers trailing over the back of Blackwood's chair—a fleeting touch that whispered of alliances yet unformed.

"Higher investment," Blackwood mused aloud, rolling the concept around like a fine wine. Doubt gnawed at him, but it was quickly being devoured by the bigger beast of greed. He envisioned his name etched alongside those reputed titans of industry.

"Exactly," Nate confirmed, his tone imbued with a hint of exclusivity. "It's the key that unlocks the next level, Bastian. You're not one to shy away from that, are you?"

A muscle twitched in Blackwood's jaw, caught between the rock of pragmatism and the hard place of his yearning for more. He imagined the accolades, the envy in his rivals' eyes... and the regret if he declined and watched others reap the windfall.

"Let me be frank," Blackwood began, voice edged with the steel that had built his empire, "I don't enjoy being rushed."

"Nor should you," Amy soothed, returning to her seat, her demeanor calm, reassuring. "But some trains only stop once at the station. This is one of those times."

"Missing out isn't in your nature," Nate concluded, the pitch in his voice rising ever so slightly, hitting the note of challenge that he knew Blackwood could never resist.

The clock continued its relentless march, a reminder that time waits for no man—not even Sebastian Blackwood. The room seemed to shrink, the walls pressing in with the weight of a decision that beckoned with the seductive call of power and prestige.

"Alright," Blackwood finally said, his voice a low rumble of capitulation mixed with excitement. "Show me what stepping up my game looks like."

The sleek mahogany table between them was a polished sea of anticipation, the reflected sheen of the overhead lights wavered like ripples under Blackwood's frown. "I'm not blind to opportunities," he said, spreading his hands wide on the tabletop as if to physically grasp the proposal. "But I've built my empire on more than just gut feelings—what are the inherent risks if I pour more into this venture?"

Nate leaned forward, his eyes locking onto Blackwood's with the intensity of a hawk. "Every investment has its risks, Bastian," he acknowledged, the timbre of his voice steady and sure. "But we've accounted for variables. We're talking about controlled risk—for someone with your acumen, it's negligible."

Amy unfolded a glossy brochure, sliding it across the table. The action was practiced, smooth—a magician revealing the trick without diminishing the allure. "We've taken every precaution," she added, pointing to the charts that showed upward trends so sharp they nearly leaped off the page. "This isn't gambling, it's strategic advancement."

Blackwood's gaze darted between the couple and the document, the gears in his mind audibly churning. He picked up the brochure, his thumb brushing over figures and forecasts, the papery whisper a stark contrast to the thunderous possibilities storming through his brain.

"Let's say I'm intrigued," Blackwood conceded, tapping the document with a rhythm that matched his quickening pulse. "But what makes this jump different? What do I gain by doubling down that I don't already have?"

"Exclusivity isn't just a word, it's a position," Nate said, emphasizing each syllable as if imparting a secret truth. "With a higher stake, you're not just an investor—you're a pioneer, part of an inner circle that redefines the market."

"Think of the access," Amy chimed in, her voice weaving visions of closed-door meetings and insider information. "Early buy-ins, preferential options, first look at emerging markets."

"Connections," Nate continued, the last piece clicking into place, "that lead to opportunities average investors wouldn't even dream of touching for quarters to come."

Blackwood leaned back, the leather chair creaking under the weight of his decision. His fingers drummed a staccato beat, echoing the thrumming in his veins. Could he really step aside and watch others leapfrog him to the summit?

"Alright," he murmured, almost to himself. "Say I'm considering it—what guarantees can you offer?"

"Your track record speaks for itself," Nate countered smoothly, "and ours is spotless. You've seen the projections, Bastian. This isn't about guarantees; it's about foresight. And you've never lacked vision."

"Or courage," Amy added, giving him a smile that could either be a dare or a promise—the line deliciously blurred.

Blackwood's reflection stared back at him from the glossy surface of the table, his eyes glinting with the old fire of conquest. Was it risk, or was it destiny calling?

The glint in Sebastian Blackwood's eyes sharpened, reflecting the shimmering skyline that sprawled beyond the penthouse window. The city was a chessboard, and he was poised to make a defining move. Inside him, something stirred—a cocktail of ambition and adrenaline that had long been his driving force.

"Imagine, Bastian," Nate's voice sliced through the silence, "a consortium of the elite, where each move forward is a stride ahead of the masses."

"An exclusive club," Amy added, the red in her hair igniting like a signal flare in the afternoon sun pouring through the blinds.

Blackwood's fingers paused their drumming as he pondered the vision they painted. He could almost hear the champagne corks popping, feel the buzz of electrifying conversations laced with power. This was more than an investment; it was a golden ticket to the upper echelons of influence.

"Who else is on board?" he questioned, the words barely a whisper, yet echoing with the gravity of unspoken promises.

"Individuals you know," Nate responded, leaning in. "Movers and shakers who recognize opportunity before it even knocks."

"Like who?" Blackwood's query came sharp, a businessman demanding facts.

"Ever heard of Jonathan Tressler?" Amy offered, casually dropping a name synonymous with success.

"Of course," Blackwood's voice betrayed nothing, but his mind raced—the Tressler touch turned ventures into goldmines.

"And Sarah Vargas," Nate continued, as casually as if discussing the weather. "Her portfolio's grown twenty percent since she upped her stake."

"Vargas? She's in too?" Blackwood couldn't mask the flicker of surprise this time. The thought of these titans already reaping rewards ignited a fire within him, melting away any remnants of hesitation.

"Let's just say, they see what you see—the potential for something groundbreaking," Amy's lips curled into a knowing smile.

Blackwood stood abruptly, pacing the length of the room, his reflection now a blur across the glass. With every step, his resolve hardened. To be part of this league, to not just witness but to shape the future—that was a chance fewer than few ever got.

"Set up a meeting," Blackwood commanded, turning sharply on his heel to face them. "I want to hear from them directly."

"Consider it done," Nate said, his phone already in hand, fingers tapping out the future.

Amy watched Blackwood, noting the shift in his stance, the squared shoulders of a man ready to conquer continents. He was all in—hook, line, and sinker.

A smirk tugged at Blackwood's lips. The game was set. The pieces were moving. And he was about to claim the king's share.

"Alright," Blackwood said aloud, his voice steadier now, resolute. "I'm ready to take this to the next level. What's our first move?"

Nate and Amy exchanged a glance—a silent celebration of victory. They had him, and they knew it.

"Welcome aboard, Sebastian," Nate said, his smile a harbinger of the thrilling journey ahead. "It's time to change the game."

"Is there a cap? A limit to what I can put in?" Blackwood's question hung in the air, both an inquiry and a dare.

"Only what you're willing to risk for unparalleled returns," Nate replied, locking eyes with the tycoon.

"Risk," the word lingered in Blackwood's mind, a familiar friend. Without risk, there was no thrill, no victory. The image of himself as a schoolyard giant flashed before his eyes—the same fearlessness that had made him a bully now fueled his empire.

"Sign me in," Blackwood said, his voice a low growl of ambition. He reached for the pen, its golden glint a symbol of the pact he was about to seal.

"Of course," Nate said, sliding the contract across the table. "Just here, and here."

Blackwood's hand hovered over the paper, the nib of the pen trembling ever so slightly. His thoughts raced—the sum he was about to commit was enormous, even for him. But the vision of his name heralded as a visionary... it eclipsed all trepidation.

The pen touched down, scratching the surface of the contract.

"History won't remember the cautious," he reminded himself. His signature began to take shape, a stroke of confidence followed by a flourish of certainty.

"Wait!" Nate's voice pierced the moment. Blackwood's pen halted mid-air, a hair's breadth from completion. "There's one last thing we need to discuss—the final perk for investors of your caliber."

"Perk?" Blackwood's heart skipped a beat. What could they possibly offer that would sweeten this pot?

"Let's just say..." Amy leaned in, her voice a whisper of intrigue, "it will make your investment seem like chump change."

"Tell me," Blackwood demanded, his desire for exclusivity overriding caution.

"Tomorrow," Nate said, standing up, "We reveal everything. Be ready for a call at 9 AM sharp."

"Tomorrow?" Blackwood repeated, the pen still poised above his destiny. The delay was unexpected, a hiccup in his rush towards greatness. Suspense coiled within him like a spring.

"Trust us," Amy said, her smile enigmatic as she gathered her things. "This is worth waiting for."

"Tomorrow," Blackwood mused, the word echoing ominously in his ears as he watched Nate and Amy depart. The contract lay before him, unsigned, a testament to the day's tension.

"Tomorrow," he whispered to the empty room, the cliffhanger of his fortune looming like a thundercloud on the horizon.

Chapter 7

Nate snapped the briefcase shut, the click echoing off the walls of their makeshift war room.

"Everything's here," he grunted, patting the case. "Bank statements, emails, the lot." His fingers drummed against the leather.

Amy swept her gaze over the spread of materials on the table—photographs, timelines, digital recordings—all meticulously organized. "We've got him, Nate. One way or another, Blackwood's going down today."

"He is," Nate affirmed, checking the secure line on his burner phone. He appreciated precision, every piece of evidence was a bullet in the chamber.

As they packed up the final pieces, Amy's keen eye caught a stray paper. She tucked it into the briefcase alongside the rest, her mind mapping out the confrontation ahead. Each document was a steppingstone toward justice for Evie and the countless others Blackwood had trampled on his climb to the top.

"Location's set?" Nate asked, snapping her from her reverie.

"Secured and soundproofed. No one will hear him even if he screams bloody murder," Amy replied, her lips curling into a smile that didn't quite reach her eyes.

"Good. Let's move out."

***

The pair navigated through the labyrinth of hallways, making their way to an unused section of the building. They arrived at a nondescript door, its paint giving no hint of the pivotal scene it was about to host.

"Here we are," Nate said as he unlocked the door, the tumblers clicking like a timer counting down. The room beyond was barren except for a sturdy table and four chairs—one for each of them, and two for pretense.

He set the briefcase down with a thud, then swept the room with a practiced glance, checking for any overlooked vulnerabilities. It had to be airtight; Blackwood was cunning, and any slip could turn the tables.

"Cameras rolling?" he questioned, pointing to the hidden devices they'd installed earlier.

"Rolling and recording," Amy confirmed, pulling a small monitor from her bag and showing Nate the feed. Their faces were grim but determined—the gravity of their mission etched into every line on their faces.

"Once he walks through that door, it's game over for Sebastian Blackwood," Amy whispered, her voice steel wrapped in velvet.

Nate nodded, feeling the weight of time spent chasing ghosts of justice. This time, though, the ghost would have a name and a face, and he wouldn't be disappearing into thin air. Not if Nate had anything to say about it.

"Let's do this," he said, clapping a hand on Amy's shoulder. Together, they took their positions on either side of the table, a united front ready to bring down a titan.

Nate's fingers drummed on the cool metal of the table, each tap echoing off the stark walls like a metronome ticking away the seconds. The room was set in shadows, save for the cone of light cast by the single lamp above them, sharpening their features into a study of anticipation. He caught Amy's eye, and they exchanged a look that said everything about what it had taken to get here—every informant's whisper, every late-night dive into encrypted files—all leading to the precipice of this moment.

"Feels like we're about to call checkmate," Amy murmured, her gaze never leaving the door. Her words were a low hum, barely audible over the thrumming silence that filled the space between the tick-tock of time.

"Doesn't it?" Nate replied, his voice equally subdued. His palms felt clammy despite the room's chill as he wiped them on his jeans under the table.

The doorknob turned with an almost imperceptible click, but to Nate, it sounded like a starting pistol. Blackwood stepped into the room, his tall frame momentarily filling the doorway before he moved forward, his eyes widening ever so slightly as he took in the sight of Nate and Amy flanking the table.

"Mr. Everhart, Mrs. Everhart," Blackwood began, a practiced smile stretching across his lips, "I must say, I wasn't expecting such... theatrics." His voice trailed off as he scanned the room, searching for clues in their carefully neutral expressions.

"Surprise is the spice of life, Bastian," Nate said with a tight smirk, watching as confusion flickered behind Blackwood's eyes. There was a slight tilt to Blackwood's head, the gears turning as he assessed the situation.

"Or is it the spice of downfall?" Amy added, her tone playful yet edged with steel. She leaned back in her chair, arms crossed, her posture casual but her eyes sharp as tacks.

"Downfall?" Blackwood echoed, his curiosity piqued. He chuckled softly, the sound hollow in the confined space. "Now you've truly piqued my interest."

"Good," Nate replied curtly, his heart pounding a fierce rhythm against his ribs. "Because you're going to want to pay close attention to what comes next."

Blackwood's initial air of amusement seemed to waver, replaced by the dawning understanding that this was not a social call or a mere business meeting. Nate could see the shift from the corner of his eye, the subtle straightening of Blackwood's spine as he prepared to face whatever came his way.

Nate leaned forward, the table's edge cold beneath his palms. "Bastian," he began, voice calm but carrying a weight that demanded attention, "we're not here for small talk."

Blackwood's smile faltered, eyes narrowing as he met Nate's unyielding gaze. Amy's fingers drummed lightly on the tabletop, a rhythmic punctuation to the gravity of the moment.

"Let's cut to the chase." Nate's words were clipped, precise. "We have evidence of your exploitation of the staff in your cleaning business. And it's time you faced the music."

"Exploitation?" Blackwood scoffed, though his composure was cracking, the facade of control slipping like sand through fingers. "You'll have to do better than vague accusations."

"Vague?" Amy chuckled darkly, pushing a thick folder across the table toward him. "There's nothing vague about this."

Inside the folder lay an array of documents, each meticulously organized and labeled. Nate watched as Blackwood's eyes flicked over the first few pages—a litany of transactions, emails, and photographs that painted a damning picture.

"Here we have testimony from your employees," Amy said, her voice slicing through the silence that had fallen over the room. "Underpaid, overworked. Forced, not only to sell their time, but their bodies. Threatened into silence."

"And here—" Nate tapped a photo where Blackwood could be seen shaking hands with a dubious character, all smiles and false bonhomie "—is you, engaging in less than savory business deals."

"Anyone can doctor photos," Blackwood retorted, but there was a tremor in his voice now, something akin to fear.

"True. But not bank records." Nate slid another sheet forward. "These are harder to fake."

Amy leaned in, her red hair a fiery banner of determination. "We've uncovered every dirty penny in your finances. It's over."

The room shrank to a battlefield of wills, Blackwood's once-imposing figure now seeming less sure, less grandiose. The documents before him were irrefutable—the product of countless hours of investigation, hacking, and surveillance. They were the nails in the coffin of his empire built on exploitation.

"Think carefully about your next move," Nate advised, an authoritative edge to his words. His mind raced, anticipating the possible fallout, always two steps ahead. This was the culmination of their work, the moment of truth, and Nate Everhart would see justice served.

Blackwood's fingers twitched, a subconscious betrayal of his unravelling composure as he reached for the damning documents. "This is preposterous," he muttered, but his voice lacked conviction.

"Is it, Bastian?" Amy's tone was ice over steel. "Evie Brooks—remember her? She came to you for a job, not for... whatever twisted entertainment you and your clients had in mind."

"Cleaning houses naked for extra tips?" Nate's brow furrowed in disgust. "That's one hell of a job description."

"It's called service customization," Blackwood snapped, attempting to mask his panic with bravado. His heart hammered—a cacophony of dread that echoed louder with each piece of evidence they laid out before him.

"Customization? You mean coercion," Amy shot back, her eyes narrowed. "You put her in a position where she felt that she had no choice."

"Never!" Blackwood slammed his palm onto the table; the impact resounded like a gavel pronouncing guilt.

"Let's not forget the others," Nate interjected, voice calm but carrying the weight of a sledgehammer. "How many more Evies out there, Bastian?"

Blackwood's mouth opened, then closed. No words came; just shallow breaths as his empire of shame loomed over him. Each document, each testimony, was a brick pulled from his fortress of deceit.

"Victims," Amy corrected herself, "Not employees. They are victims of your exploitation."

"Allegations," Blackwood clung to the word like a life raft in tempestuous waters. "I'll see you in court."

"Will you?" Nate challenged. The room felt colder now, sterile, as if waiting for judgment to cleanse it. "Or will the court see these?"

He held up another photo—Evie, eyes hollow, a forced smile failing to hide her fear. It was a silent scream, an indictment more powerful than any words could ever be.

"Enough," Blackwood whispered, the fight leaving him in one long, defeated exhale. His shoulders slumped, the posture of a man who knew his reckoning was at hand.

Blackwood's eyes, once the sharp beacons of a predator, now darted around the room, seeking an exit that wasn't there. Nate leaned forward, his fingers steepled, the ghost of a smirk playing on his lips.

"You owe Evie," he said, voice as steady as bedrock. "Not just apologies. Restitution."

"Monetary?" Blackwood's voice cracked like thin ice underfoot.

"Every penny she should've been paid," Amy replied, her tone slicing through the air. "And then some for emotional damages."

"Damages?" The word seemed foreign on Blackwood's tongue, the concept alien to his world where currency was power and empathy a liability.

"Did you think we'd stop at exposing you?" Nate asked, his eyebrows arching in mock surprise. His hand slid across the table, nudging a folder closer to Blackwood. "This is about making it right."

"Making it..." Blackwood's voice trailed off. He looked between the couple, his usual command eroding before their unyielding resolve.

"Justice," Amy enunciated the word like a verdict.

"Justice," Nate echoed, the term solidifying into something tangible within the confines of the room.

Blackwood's hands trembled as he reached for the folder, the papers inside holding the weight of his sins. He scanned the contents, each line another nail in his coffin of greed.

"Think of it as an investment," Nate suggested. "In decency. Something your portfolio's been lacking."

"Decency doesn't pay dividends," Blackwood retorted, but the defiance in his voice was hollow, eaten away by the acid of truth.

"Neither does exploitation. Not in the long run." Amy stood up, her silhouette framed by the stark lighting, casting long shadows over Blackwood who appeared smaller somehow, diminished.

"Is this what you want?" Blackwood's question was directed at Nate, but it was Amy who answered.

"It's not about what we want," she said. "It's about what's owed. To Evie. To every person you've stepped on to climb higher."

"Or what?" The challenge crept back into Blackwood's tone, a last-ditch effort to regain ground.

"Or we let the world see you for who you really are," Nate replied. "No more hiding behind lawyers and payouts."

"Your move, Bastian." Amy's words hung in the air, a gauntlet thrown down at Blackwood's feet.

Blackwood slumped in his chair, the realization dawning upon him that the game had changed. No longer the player, he was now the pawn, cornered and outmaneuvered. The power he so relished to wield had slipped through his fingers, now firmly in the grasp of those he'd underestimated.

"Fine," he conceded, the word forced out like the last gasp of a deflating ego.

Nate's gaze didn't waver; it was the look of a man who'd seen battles and bore the scars of a deeper war. This victory was a step, one of many, in a fight for the underdog—a fight that he'd pledged himself to long ago.

"Good choice." Amy's response was devoid of gloating, her satisfaction found only in the righteousness of their cause.

She pointed to the cameras. "These are recording audio too. We have enough to hang you."

Sebastian Blackwood, the once unshakeable titan of industry, looked smaller somehow, penned in by the truth that now lined the walls around him. The photographs, the emails, the testimonies—they all spoke of a legacy far removed from the grandeur he had envisioned for himself. He shifted in his chair, the leather creaking under the weight of his sudden vulnerability.

"Look at their faces," Amy said, her voice cutting through the silence, sharp and precise. "This is your handiwork."

His eyes flicked toward the images she indicated—a collage of tired eyes and worn hands, all belonging to people who had served beneath him, invisible in their servitude. A pang of something unfamiliar twisted in Blackwood's gut. Was it guilt? It gnawed at him, this new sensation, burrowing deeper with every second he spent trapped in his own web of deceit.

"Didn't think it would catch up to you?" Nate's question was rhetorical, a verbal jab to keep Blackwood off balance.

He wanted to lash out, to regain his footing with a well-placed word or a dismissive scoff, but the energy for such posturing had drained from him, leaving only the stark reality of the situation. Sebastian Blackwood, for once, had nothing to say.

"Evie trusted you," Amy continued, her gaze unwavering. "And you exploited that trust. You exploited all of them."

Her words were like blows, each one landing with precision.

There was no escaping it. The evidence was irrefutable, a shining mirror reflecting a portrait of a man he could no longer recognize. "What do you want from me?"

"Everything you've taken from them." Nate's demand was simple, yet it carried the weight of mountains.

"Restitution," Amy added, pushing a document across the table toward him. "Monetary compensation for the harm done. And it starts with Evie."

Blackwood reached for a pen with a shaky hand, his signature, once an emblem of power, now a token of surrender. As the pen scratched across the paper, each stroke felt like an etching on the tablet of his soul—acknowledging the harm, accepting the consequences.

"Is this what justice feels like?" he asked, the words barely audible, more to himself than to his accusers. It was a question born from the ruins of his arrogance, uttered by a man who saw, perhaps for the first time, the world beyond the walls of his own making.

"Yes," Nate replied, firm and without malice. "It's a start."

Blackwood nodded, a fragment of the defiance that had once defined him flaring and then fading in the span of a heartbeat. He looked up at Nate and Amy, seeing them not as enemies, but as harbingers of a truth he could no longer deny.

As the papers exchanged hands, a chapter closed in the book of Sebastian Blackwood. Maybe, just maybe, another was beginning—one where the ink told a different story.

The room hummed with a stillness that seemed to echo the gravity of what had just transpired. Blackwood's hand, now devoid of its former tremor, hovered over the tablet, the digital numbers punching in with an air of finality. Nate and Amy watched as the amount keyed in matched the figure they had demanded—a substantial sum that would change Evie's life irreversibly.

"Transfer," Blackwood said simply, pressing the button.

"Confirmation sent," replied the banking app, impersonal and efficient in its delivery of justice.

Amy let out a soft breath she hadn't realized she was holding, and Nate felt the tension drain from his shoulders. The satisfaction tickled at him like the first drops of rain after a relentless drought, soaking into the parched ground of their long-fought battle.

"Evie will get every penny by tomorrow morning," Nate affirmed, his voice steady as he held Blackwood's gaze.

"Good." Blackwood's reply was almost inaudible, but it carved through the silence, marking a promise kept.

***

As they gathered the documents that had laid bare Blackwood's misdeeds, Amy couldn't help but think of Evie's face—the relief that would wash over her when she heard the news. She imagined Evie's hands trembling as she opened her account to find redemption spelled out in digits—a vindication no one could take away from her.

"Never thought I'd see the day," Nate mused aloud, a half-smile tugging at the corner of his mouth.

"Me neither," Amy agreed, the corners of her eyes crinkling with a rare lightness. "But we did it, Nate. We actually did it."

Their eyes met, a silent conversation flowing between them. They had bent the arc of the universe towards justice, even if just by an inch. But sometimes, Nate knew, an inch was enough to topple empires.

"Let's go home, Amelia." His words were more than an invitation; they were a benediction for the end of one journey and the quiet prelude to whatever lay ahead.

"Home," she echoed, allowing herself the luxury of thinking about a bottle of wine and the comfort of their couch. But then, there was always another case, another Evie waiting in the wings. For now, though, they would savor the victory.

"By the way," Nate added, pausing at the door. "You were brilliant today."

Amy's smile was all the answer he needed as they stepped out of the room, leaving behind a man and his reckoning. They walked through the deserted corridors, side by side, their strides brimming with the weariness and exhilaration that only comes from having fought the good fight.

"Justice feels pretty damn good," Amy said, breaking the silence.

Nate chuckled. "It does, doesn't it? And so does working with you."

"Likewise," she replied, nudging him playfully with her shoulder. "Partners in crime—"

"—and justice," Nate finished, as they pushed through the doors and into the cool embrace of the night, the city lights winking like distant stars, silent witnesses to the balance they had restored, if only for a moment.

CHECKMATE

The crisp air outside prickled against Nate's skin as he and Amy emerged from the building, the night sky a blanket of dark velvet pierced by the city's shimmering lights. The sense of satisfaction that had buoyed them moments before now mingled with an undercurrent of unease. They had won a battle, sure, but the war was far from over.

They slipped into the car, the interior holding the faint scent of leather and coffee. As Nate started the engine, the dashboard's glow illuminated their faces, casting shadows that flickered like those of a fading fire.

"Home then?" Amy's voice was steady, but Nate caught the slight tremor of adrenaline still coursing through her veins.

"Home." He affirmed, pulling away from the curb. In the rearview mirror, the building where they'd faced down Blackwood loomed, a silent monument to the evening's confrontation.

Chapter 8

Nate sank into the plush embrace of their living room couch, a fortress of comfort starkly contrasting the world they had just turned on its head. The dim glow of lamplight cast shadows across Amy's face, accentuating the relief that softened her usually sharp features.

"Can you believe it?" Nate's voice was a low rumble, mingling with the hum of the quiet house. "We actually pulled it off."

Amy leaned back, the leather creaking under her weight as she propped her feet on the coffee table. "I can believe it, because we did it," she said, a wry smile playing on her lips.

Nate watched the firelight flicker in her eyes, mirroring the triumph he felt thrumming in his veins. The plan had been risky, threading the needle between justice and retribution, but Evie's haunted gaze, once so burdened, now held glimmers of hope.

His fingers drummed on the armrest, beating to the racing thoughts in his head. They had dived into the mire of Blackwood's corruption, sifted through the filth, and emerged victorious for Evie. It was a win—not just for them, but for every underdog who'd suffered at the hands of the powerful.

"Justice for Evie," Amy murmured, as if she'd plucked the thought right from his mind. Her eyes met his, fierce and proud. "After everything, she deserves this peace."

"Exactly." Nate's response was immediate, decisive. He stood up and started pacing, the kinetic energy of the moment too much for stillness. "And we gave it to her. We dismantled part of Blackwood's empire today."

Amy nodded, her red hair catching the light like flames. She was the detail, the precision behind their operation, while he... he was the spark. Together, they were an unstoppable force.

"Though, I must admit," Amy continued, breaking into his reverie, "there's something deliciously ironic about using his own tricks against him."

"Poetic justice?" Nate suggested with a chuckle, stopping to look down at her.

"Best kind," she shot back, her grin infectious.

He joined her laughter, feeling the tension of the past weeks begin to unravel. In the sanctuary of their home, they were more than just partners in crime; they were two halves of a whole, bound by shared ideals and an unyielding desire to tilt the scales in favor of the innocent.

"Here's to us, then," Nate said, extending his hand to help Amy up from the couch. "To justice, to peace...and to whatever comes next."

"Whatever comes next," Amy echoed, accepting his hand and rising to stand beside him. They shared a look, one charged with the understanding that their crusade was far from over.

But tonight, they had won a battle, and that victory was sweet.

The silence that followed their toast was comfortable at first, hanging between Nate and Amy like a well-earned reprieve. But as the minutes ticked by, the quiet began to swell with unspoken thoughts, growing heavy in the air.

Nate let out a long sigh, his gaze fixed on the dying embers of the fireplace. "You ever think about what we do? The lines we cross?" He glanced at Amy, the flickering light casting shadows across her face.

"Every time," she admitted softly, tucking a strand of red hair behind her ear. "But then I remember the faces of those we've helped. And I wonder... can there be morality in deceit?"

"Deceit for justice's sake," Nate mused, his voice trailing off. He couldn't shake the image of Blackwood's stunned expression when they'd pulled the rug out from under him. A part of Nate thrived on the thrill, but another, deeper part recoiled at the deception.

Amy leaned back against the couch, her green eyes reflecting a world-weary knowledge. "It's a paradox, isn't it? Using the enemy's weapons against them. But if we don't, who will stop the Blackwoods of this world?"

"Right," he murmured, pushing himself off the mantle. He crossed the room to sit beside her, the floorboards creaking under his weight. There was solace in her presence, but also a reminder of the cost. They'd spent sleepless nights plotting, days buried in lies, all to bring down one untouchable titan.

"Sometimes, I feel like we're teetering on the edge," Nate confessed, rubbing at his tired eyes. "What if we fall into the same abyss we're fighting?"

Amy reached over, her hand finding his. "We won't," she assured him, though her voice wavered just enough to betray her own uncertainty.

They sat there, hands clasped, the silence now filled with the echo of their doubts. The emotional toll was etched into their weary postures, the strain of living double lives pulling at them like a riptide.

"Blackwood looked broken, didn't he?" Amy said after a moment, her thumb absently stroking Nate's hand. It was a small touch, but it held the weight of shared experience, the bond of countless battles fought side by side.

"Broken," Nate repeated, the word tasting bitter on his tongue. "Does breaking a man like that make us any better than him?"

"Justice isn't always clean," she replied, her voice firm despite the tremor Nate knew only he could hear. "And guilt... it shows we still have our humanity. That has to count for something, doesn't it?"

"Maybe." Nate's reply was faint, almost lost in the crackling of the fire. He leaned his head back against the couch, closing his eyes as he tried to reconcile the rush of victory with the gnawing sense of culpability.

"We did what we had to do." Amy's conviction was a lifeline in the darkness of his doubts. "For Evie, and for all the others who can't fight back."

"Did we?" Nate's question wasn't meant to challenge, but to seek assurance. Opening his eyes, he found Amy watching him, her expression a mixture of determination and empathy.

"Absolutely," she said, squeezing his hand tighter. It was an anchor, a promise that no matter how rough the seas, they would navigate them together.

"Then let's make sure it was worth it," Nate resolved, the last vestiges of hesitation dissipating like smoke up the chimney. They were in this together, and that unity fortified him.

"Agreed," Amy said, her lips curving into a smile that didn't quite reach her eyes. She was as tired as he was, the shadows beneath her eyes testament to the emotional toll of their crusade against Blackwood.

"Every action has its cost," Nate mused aloud, staring into the flames as if they held answers. "We've paid ours in sleepless nights and a conscience heavier than when we started."

"True," she conceded, leaning her head on his shoulder, her fiery mane spilling over him like a protective shroud. "But remember the lives we've untangled from his web? That's our currency, Nate. It's not just about what we've taken from Blackwood; it's about what we've given back to those he hurt."

"Restitution over retribution, huh?" Nate quipped weakly, trying to lift the gravity from their conversation. Amy chuckled, the sound warm against the cool silence that had settled around them.

"Sounds like something out of a superhero comic," she teased, nudging him gently.

"Maybe we need capes," Nate joked back, though the laughter didn't quite mask the fatigue etched in his voice.

"Only if they're bulletproof," Amy retorted wryly, but her gaze softened as she looked up at him. "Nate, I know you. You wouldn't have done any of this if you didn't believe it was absolutely necessary. You fought for your country; now we're fighting for justice in the shadows where laws don't always reach."

"Sometimes I miss the clarity of orders and objectives," he confessed, the soldier in him wrestling with the vigilante he'd become.

"Life wasn't meant to be black and white," Amy reminded him, her fingers tracing patterns on the back of his hand. "What matters is that we're making a difference, even if it's one that'll never be recognized by medals or parades."

"Anonymity has its perks," Nate said, a ghost of his usual smirk playing on his lips. "No paparazzi, for starters."

"Or cleaning up after Blackwood's mess," Amy added, and they shared a look that said they both understood the irony. They'd turned the tables on a man who outsourced his dirty work, only to find themselves knee-deep in the cleanup of his corruption.

"Tomorrow's another day," Nate finally said, rising from his seat. He extended a hand to Amy, pulling her up into his embrace. "We'll figure out where to go from here. Together."

"Always together," Amy agreed, her arms winding around him. In that moment, the weight on their shoulders seemed a little lighter, shared between them.

As the fire dwindled to embers, Nate and Amy stood in silent solidarity, the warmth between them a balm against the chill of doubt. Tomorrow would indeed come, and with it, the next chapter in their unorthodox pursuit of justice. But for now, they found solace in the quiet reflection that, despite the moral ambiguity of their world, they were each other's unwavering certainty.

Nate traced the wood grain of the coffee table, a labyrinthine pattern that seemed to echo the complexity of their predicament. His fingers paused at a knot in the surface, emblematic perhaps of the ethical knot they now faced. Amy watched him, her own hands wrapped around a mug, though the tea within had long since lost its steam.

"Blackwood deserved every bit of what we dished out," Nate said, breaking the silence, his voice a low rumble that seemed to carry the weight of their actions. "Every scheme, every lie he's spun, came back to haunt him."

Amy's gaze lifted from the stagnant tea leaves to meet Nate's resolute stare. "But have we become reflections of him in the process?" she countered. "Deception for deception's sake?"

"Justice isn't always clean, Ames." Nate rose and paced before the dying fire, his military-honed posture rigid against the shadows dancing on the wall. "We used the tools at our disposal. The same ones he used to exploit those with no voice."

She set the mug down, the clink of ceramic on wood punctuating her sigh. "I know... I just worry about the lines we cross. How they change us."

"Change is inevitable," Nate argued, stopping to face her. "But unlike Blackwood, our compass points toward something greater than ourselves."

"Perhaps." Amy leaned forward, elbows resting on her knees as her red hair cascaded over her shoulders like a fiery shroud. "Yet, it doesn't absolve us of the harm inflicted. We played God with his fate."

"God? No." Nate's chuckle was humorless. "More like the scales of justice—balancing the equation." He approached her, knelt down, and took her hands in his. "We did what the law couldn't."

"Or wouldn't," Amy added softly, allowing the warmth from his hands to seep into hers. She searched his eyes, seeking the conviction she once saw there. It flickered, but it was shadowed by questions that mirrored her own.

"Exactly," Nate said, squeezing her hands gently, a tacit acknowledgment of their shared uncertainty. "We're not heroes, Amy. But we're certainly not villains. We've merely stepped into the gray where the black and white of morality blurs."

"Gray is a dangerous color—it can so easily darken," Amy whispered, her thoughts churning like the embers in the hearth. "And what then? When does the scale tip too far?"

"We recalibrate." Nate's voice was firm, decisive. "We stay vigilant. We hold each other accountable."

"Accountability..." Amy echoed, a ghost of a smile touching her lips. "It's what started this whole thing. Holding Blackwood accountable."

"Darn tooting." Nate stood, pulling her up with him. "And we'll continue to do so—for him, for others like him. We won't let the darkness win."

"Even if we sometimes feel it nipping at our heels," Amy quipped, a hint of her natural levity surfacing despite the gravity of their conversation.

"Especially then," Nate affirmed, his eyes gleaming with the spark that had first ignited their partnership. "Because that's when we fight the hardest."

"Fight and keep fighting," Amy mused, her spirit rallying with his. "Just promise me one thing, Nate."

"Anything."

"Next time, let's try for a little less cloak and dagger and a bit more transparency. For our own sanity's sake."

"Agreed," Nate said, a genuine smile finally carving through the tension. "Transparency it is—starting with us. Always honest with each other, no matter how murky the waters get."

"Deal." Amy nodded, sealing their pact with a firm grip of his hand. Together, steadfast in their resolve, they stood ready to face whatever moral quandaries lay ahead, united in purpose and fortified by the trust that bound them.

The glow from the fireplace cast a flickering light on Nate's face as he stared into the leaping flames, his brows furrowed in contemplation. The quiet crackle of burning wood was a stark contrast to the storm that raged within him.

"Blackwood's empire," Amy began, her voice low, slicing through the silence of their cozy living room. "If he goes down, it's not just him—it's a whole network. Employees, investors... lives upended."

"Collateral damage," Nate muttered, turning his attention from the fire to meet her gaze. He stood and paced, restless energy coursing through him. "But how many more would suffer if we did nothing? How long before his greed devours another innocent?"

Amy watched him, tracing the familiar tension in his jawline. "I know. It's just—" She hesitated, her fingers nervously tugging at a loose thread on the armrest. "The fallout could be massive. If our involvement gets out, we'd be pariahs, or worse."

"Then we make sure it never does," Nate said, halting before the mantelpiece, his hands bracing against it. His military past had ingrained a tactical mindset, always thinking two steps ahead. "We covered our tracks, used every trick in the book. Blackwood's taken hits before; he'll weather this storm too. Maybe even learn something."

"Optimistic," Amy mused with a wry smile that didn't quite reach her eyes. Her background in investigative journalism had taught her that men like Blackwood rarely changed. They just got better at hiding their sins.

"Realistic," Nate countered, the corner of his mouth lifting briefly. "He's got resources, but so do we. And we've got something he'll never have—"

"Each other." Amy finished the thought, rising to join him by the fireplace.

"Exactly." Nate reached out, his fingers intertwining with hers. The contact sparked a connection, grounding them both amidst the uncertainty.

"Us against the world, huh?" Amy squeezed his hand, drawing strength from the familiarity of his touch. "That's how this all started. But what if it's also what ends us?"

Nate's eyes searched hers, the humor fading to reveal a depth of concern. "This mission... it's pushed us to our limits. Made us question our own ethics."

"Made us lie, cheat, and sneak around like characters in a bad spy novel," Amy said, though her attempt at levity fell flat. "It's thrilling, terrifying... but I can't shake the feeling that every step we take together might be one step further apart."

"Hey." Nate cupped her cheek gently, compelling her to look at him. "Nothing about this is easy. But every choice we've made, we've made together. That counts for something."

"Does it make us stronger, or just more adept at deception?" Amy's voice trembled slightly, baring a vulnerability she usually kept shielded.

"Stronger," Nate asserted, conviction steeling his tone. "Because we're transparent with each other. We don't hide behind lies—not with one another."

"True." A faint smile returned to Amy's lips, her green eyes reflecting the fire's warmth. "We're a team. In the thick of it, when everything's on the line, I trust you. Implicitly."

"And I trust you," Nate affirmed, leaning in closer. "Whatever happens with Blackwood, whatever consequences come, we'll face them. Together."

"Promise me something?" Amy asked, her expression earnest.

"Anything."

"Never let this—the danger, the adrenaline—become more important than 'us.'"

"Never," Nate vowed, sealing his promise with a kiss that held the weight of shared resolve.

Nate stared into the dying embers of the fireplace, the glow casting a flickering light across his furrowed brow. He could feel Amy's gaze on him, heavy with unspoken thoughts. Their living room, once a sanctuary of peace, now seemed to echo with the gravity of their recent actions.

"Did we do the right thing?" Amy broke the silence, her voice barely above a whisper. Her fingers toyed with a loose thread on the arm of the sofa, a small but telling sign of her inner turmoil.

He turned to her, studying her face in the half-light. "We stopped a man who ruined lives without a second thought," Nate said, his words measured. "The law couldn't touch Blackwood, but we did."

"Yet," she countered, her red hair casting a fiery halo in the fire's glow, "in doing so, we've stepped into a moral gray area. We used deceit, manipulation... I fear what that says about us."

Nate leaned forward, elbows on knees, hands clasped together. "It says we're willing to do what's necessary. Our methods may be questionable, but our intention—to protect the innocent—is pure."

Amy sighed, pulling her legs up onto the couch and wrapping her arms around them. "Intention doesn't always equate to justification. Every move we made was calculated, yes, but can we honestly say there was no other way? No cleaner path?"

"Clean paths don't always lead to justice, Ames. You know that better than anyone." Nate's gaze hardened as he recalled all those who had suffered at Blackwood's hands. "We navigated a maze designed by the corrupt and came out the other side."

She met his eyes, her own reflecting the flicker of doubt that danced within. "But are we still the good guys if we start using the villain's playbook?"

"Good guys..." Nate murmured, a wry smile tugging at the corner of his mouth. He rose from his seat and walked over to the window, peering out into the darkness. "That term lost its simplicity a long time ago. Maybe it's not about being good or bad. It's about balance—tipping the scales when they've been unjustly weighted."

"Like Robin Hood?" Amy asked, a hint of humor threading through her uncertainty.

"Exactly." Nate turned from the window, the shadows playing across his strong features. "Robin Hood had to become an outlaw to restore what was taken. We've done the same."

"Restoration..." Amy whispered, rolling the word around as if tasting it for the first time. She unfolded herself from the couch and joined Nate by the window. "Perhaps that's where we find our moral compass."

"Perhaps," Nate agreed, wrapping an arm around her shoulders. "We restore what's been broken, protect those who can't protect themselves. It's not perfect, Amy, but it's something we can stand behind."

"Even if it costs us?" Amy looked up at him, searching his face for assurance.

"Even then." Nate's voice was firm, resolute. "Because if we stand by and do nothing, knowing what we know, then we're part of the problem."

"Then let's be part of the solution," Amy decided, a newfound determination lifting her chin. "Together, we'll keep the scales balanced."

"Agreed," Nate nodded, feeling the weight of their decision settle firmly between them. "For justice, for balance... for us."

Nate's gaze lingered on the cityscape beyond the glass, skyscrapers standing like silent sentinels in the night. The world outside was unaware of the quiet revolution brewing within the walls of their modest home.

"New cases..." Amy mused aloud, her voice a gentle prod to his thoughts. "There are others out there, Nate. Others who need what we do."

He turned to face her, the streetlights casting an amber glow over her determined expression. Her eyes were the color of ambition, of fires stoked by injustice and the fierce desire to make things right.

"Like that whistleblower from the energy sector," he said, the idea igniting something within him. "And the single mother being evicted because of some corporate landlord's greed."

"Exactly." Amy stepped closer, her movements decisive. "We have the skills, Nate. We can expose them, hold them accountable."

The air between them crackled with shared purpose. He envisioned the anonymous tip-offs, the carefully orchestrated leaks to the press, each move a calculated strike against corruption.

"Let's do it," Nate declared, his ethical hacker's heart beating in tandem with the drum of justice. "Let's be their shield."

"Let's be their sword," Amy countered, her smile sharp and bright.

Amy reached for his hand, her grip solid and real, an anchor in the tumultuous sea they navigated together. They didn't need words; their resolve was a language unto itself.

Their reflections stared back at them from the dark windowpane. As the city lights flickered like distant stars, Nate and Amy shared a moment of quiet reflection, feeling a sense of closure and contentment.

"We've made an impact, haven't we?" Amy's voice was soft, almost reverent.

"More than we'll ever know," Nate replied, his tone edged with pride. "And we'll keep making it."

The clock's minute hand inched forward, slicing the silence with its rhythmic ticking—a relentless reminder of time slipping away. Nate's gaze was fixed on it, feeling each tick mark another step in their journey.

"Tick-tock, life's clock," Amy murmured, humor dancing in her tone despite the fatigue etching her features. "What's on your mind?"

"Blackwood," he said, his voice a low rumble, mirroring his brooding thoughts. "And all the others like him."

She leaned over, pressing her lips to his temple in a brief, tender kiss that held promises of solace. "We'll get them, one by one."

Nate turned to face her, his dark eyes searching hers. "The path we're on—it's not exactly straight and narrow."

"Since when have we ever walked the beaten track?" Amy quipped, but her smile wavered under the weight of unspoken concerns.

He stood up, pacing the room with restless energy. The floorboards creaked beneath his steps, voicing their own quiet protest. "I know," he admitted, pausing to run a hand through his hair. "But the line between justice and vigilantism is thinning."

"Isn't it always?" Amy rose to join him, her movements a silent symphony of determination. "We walk it carefully, Nate. We always have."

"Too carefully?" He questioned, facing her. His expression was a tumult of conviction and doubt.

"Care is what sets us apart from the Blackwoods of this world," she countered, her hands finding his. "We care about the consequences, about the Evies whose lives hang in the balance."

"True," Nate conceded, squeezing her fingers gently. "But at what cost to us? To what we hold dear?"

"Is there a price too high for doing the right thing?" Amy asked, her voice soft but unwavering.

He didn't answer immediately, contemplating her words as they echoed within him. Finally, he nodded slowly. "No, there isn't. But that doesn't mean I don't worry about the toll it takes on you, on us."

"Hey," she lifted his chin, forcing him to meet her gaze. "We're in this together, remember? You and me, against whatever darkness comes our way."

"Against the darkness..." he repeated, the phrase solidifying something within him. His chest rose and fell with a deep breath, steadying his resolve.

"Exactly." Amy released his chin, only to wrap her arms around him. "Together, we shine brighter."

In the embrace of her arms, Nate allowed a moment of vulnerability. The comfort of their home enveloped them, a safe haven from the chaos they willingly plunged into. Tomorrow could bring new challenges, new evils to confront. But tonight, they had each other.

"Let's keep shining then," Nate whispered, pulling back to look at her once more. His lips curved into a small, resolute smile—a mirror of her own.

"Like stars in the night sky," Amy agreed, her eyes sparkling with fierce joy.

The stillness of the night was punctuated by the rhythmic ticking of the clock, its deep chimes resonating through the comfortable living room where Nate and Amy sat. They were perched on opposite ends of their plush sofa, a space charged with the electricity of their recent victory. The warm glow of the table lamp cast shadows that danced across Nate's face, highlighting his thoughtful expression as he broke the silence.

"Did we go too far?" Nate asked, the question hanging in the air like smoke from an extinguished candle.

Amy shifted, her posture as precise as the way she approached their plans—meticulously, unerringly. "We did what was necessary, Nate," she replied, her voice a blend of conviction and the barest hint of trepidation.

Nate drummed his fingers on the leather-bound book on the coffee table, the taps echoing his internal struggle. He had seen things in the military that would sear the soul, but this was different. This was personal. The lines between right and wrong blurred when they started playing judge and jury.

"Justice isn't always clean-cut," he muttered to himself, feeling the weight of their actions settle in his chest.

Amy leaned forward, her eyes scanning his features, reading him as easily as one of her case files. "We stopped Blackwood. That has to count for something."

"Does it?" Nate rose, pacing in front of the window, the moonlight casting him in stark relief. His mind was a battlefield, strategy against conscience. In the grand scheme, they were the lesser of two evils, but that didn't make them saints.

"Look at the evidence," Amy insisted, her journalistic instincts kicking in. "Blackwood ruined lives. We restored balance."

"By deceiving, hacking, manipulating?" He stopped, facing her, his silhouette sharp against the curtains.

"By doing what others couldn't," Amy countered, standing to meet him eye to eye. "Or wouldn't."

He knew she was right; that was why they made such an effective team. Her unwavering focus complemented his broader vision. Yet, doubt was a persistent adversary, creeping into his thoughts like a virus.

"Maybe." Nate's response was clipped, a reflection of his inner turmoil.

"Listen to me, Nate Everhart," Amy said, her red hair a fiery halo in the lamplight. "We've come this far together. You with your hacker's heart and me with my pen sharper than any sword. We're fixing the broken parts of the world, piece by piece."

"Pen and hacker, huh?" A ghost of a grin flickered across Nate's face, the tension in his shoulders easing ever so slightly.

"An unstoppable combination," Amy affirmed, touching his arm gently, grounding him.

"Unstoppable," he echoed, allowing the truth of her words to fortify the resolve that had momentarily wavered.

"Let's get some rest," Nate said, the decision clear in his voice.

"Rest sounds good," Amy replied, a soft smile gracing her lips as she took his hand, leading them both towards the stairs.

Chapter 9

Evie twirled the keys around her finger, a metallic dance that matched the gleam in her eyes. The one-bedroom apartment was modest, but it was hers—no longer would she endure the humiliating demands of clients or the oppressive grip of Bastian's employment. Fresh paint adorned the walls, a defiant shade of sunflower yellow that seemed to mock the drabness of her past. It was an improvement born from the ashes of servitude, a sanctuary pieced together with resilience.

"Never thought I'd feel this good about spending money on coasters," Evie mused aloud, arranging a set of geometric stone coasters on her brand-new coffee table. Each piece felt like a declaration, a tangible assertion of independence. She had picked them out herself, no longer needing to sift through cast-offs or accept hand-me-downs that carried the weight of someone else's history.

As she fluffed the teal throw pillows for the umpteenth time, the doorbell rang—a crisp chime heralding the arrival of more than just a visitor. It signaled the arrival of possibility. Evie opened the door to the delivery men, who grunted under the weight of a sleek new bookshelf.

"Right over there, thanks," she directed, pointing to the spot she had measured thrice. They shuffled and maneuvered, until with a final heave, the shelf was nestled against the wall, a backbone for Evie's growing collection of literature and knick-knacks.

"Sign here, Ma'am," one of the men said, extending a clipboard towards her. The title 'Ma'am' sat strangely on her ears, a reminder that she was no longer seen as a mere fixture in someone's home, but the mistress of her own domain.

"Perfect," she said as they left, her signature trailing behind them like a flag planted on newfound territory.

She slid her fingers across the polished wood, each book spine she placed into the cubbies whispering stories of fresh starts and adventures yet lived. Her thoughts raced ahead, imagining the hours she would spend curled up on her new sofa, lost in pages that promised escapades and heroics far removed from her own battles.

"Wow, I actually own novels now, not just dust jackets," Evie chuckled to herself, running a hand through her hair. It was a small victory, but it was hers.

There was a method to her madness, a deliberate reclaiming of space and self. She arranged her possessions with care, an antithesis to the haphazard existence she had been forced into before. Everything had its place, every choice was her own—down to the quirky owl-shaped vase that now occupied a place of honor on the mantlepiece.

"Who knew freedom had a color scheme?" she quipped, stepping back to admire the harmony of hues that filled her living room. Gone were the days of scrubbing floors on hands and knees, replaced by the quiet dignity of arranging her life, one cushion, one frame at a time.

The sense of security wrapped around her like the softest blanket, comforting and warm. With every purchase, every decision made, Evie wove a tapestry of autonomy, vibrant threads in a narrative she was finally the author of.

The morning sun infiltrated Evie's kitchen, its rays playing tag with the motes of flour suspended in the air. She was enveloped in the sweet aroma of baking bread, a rich, yeasty scent that promised comfort and sustenance. The oven timer dinged, and she pulled out a golden loaf, the crust crackling as it met the cooler air.

She set the bread aside to cool, relishing the sizzle and pop from the pan where strips of bacon flirted with caramelization. "Cooking's its own kind of freedom, isn't it?" The question was more for herself than anyone else, and she smiled at the thought.

Outside, the park was coming alive; dog walkers, joggers, and early risers crisscrossed the green expanse. A decision made, she slid off her apron and stepped into her sneakers.

"Fresh air beats recycled grievances any day," she said, locking the door behind her. The breeze caught her hair, and she brushed it back, her steps syncing with the heartbeat of the city.

The park greeted her with a symphony of natural and urban sounds—the twitter of birdsong, the laughter of children, the distant hum of traffic. Evie inhaled deeply, the smell of freshly cut grass mingling with a hint of coffee from a nearby café.

"Never knew how much I needed this," she confessed to a passing squirrel, which cocked its head as if considering her words. She chuckled, feeling a kinship with the creature's curiosity.

She wandered aimlessly, her path a meandering trail through the new day. With every stride, there was a lightness in her chest, a buoyancy that had been absent for too long. She wasn't running from something; she was walking towards everything.

"Life's not all about dodging shadows," she thought, watching a family play fetch with their dog. For the first time in a long while, the prospect of tomorrow didn't weigh heavy on her mind—it danced, inviting and bright.

Returning home, Evie poured herself a glass of water, the ice cubes clinking cheerfully against the sides. The bread beckoned, and she tore off a piece, the steam curling up like a whispered secret between old friends. She took a bite, the flavors bursting with honesty and hope.

"Simple pleasures, huh?" she mused aloud. "Guess they're the real luxuries." The bread was proof, tangible evidence of life's most basic joys rediscovered, savored without fear or compromise.

***

The glint of chrome and the scent of oil greeted Evie as she entered the garage-turned-workshop, a stark contrast to the sterile environment she'd been accustomed to. The shelves were lined with jars of screws, nuts, and bolts, each meticulously labeled in her own handwriting. In the center stood a classic motorcycle, its once dull frame now boasting a fresh coat of fiery red paint that seemed to pulse with life.

Evie pushed the button to open the garage door, allowing a sliver of sunlight to pierce through the dimly lit space. She squinted as her eyes adjusted to the sudden brightness. In the distance, she spotted a sleek sedan pulling up to the curb and two figures emerging from it. As they made their way towards her, Evie recognized Nate and Amy, their smiles reaching their eyes as they approached her with eager steps.

"Never thought I'd see you wielding a wrench," Nate's voice echoed off the concrete walls as he crossed the threshold, a grin spreading across his face.

"Neither did I," Evie replied without looking up, focusing on tightening a bolt. "But there's something honest about it—taking something broken and making it whole again." Her hands, once only used for scrubbing and cleaning to others' twisted standards, now worked with purpose, assembling and creating. She was rebuilding more than just an engine; she was piecing together the fragments of her past into something new.

"Looks like you've found your rhythm," Amy chimed in, stepping beside Nate, her eyes reflecting pride.

"Thanks to you both," Evie said, setting down the wrench. She wiped her brow, leaving a smudge of grease that signified hard work and progress. "You gave me the tools to start over, not just this..." she gestured to the bike, "...but a real chance at life."

"Speaking of starting over," Nate began, unfolding a brochure he pulled from his jacket pocket. "Thought you might want to check this out—a coding bootcamp. It's right up your alley, considering your knack for puzzles and patterns."

Evie took the brochure, her eyes scanning the bold letters and vibrant imagery promising a future in tech. "It's perfect," she breathed out, the possibilities already scripting themselves in her mind. A new hobby, or perhaps a career—something she could own completely.

"Already enrolled you," Amy confessed with a wink. "Class starts Monday."

"Enrolled me?" Evie's heart skipped. It was one thing to dream, another to have someone believe in you enough to make it reality. "I don't know what to say..."

"Start with 'hello world'," Nate joked, earning a chuckle from both women.

"Look," Evie began, her voice thick with emotion, "I can't ever repay you for what you've done for me."

"Hey, we don't do this for payback," Amy interjected, her tone gentle. "We do it because it's right."

"Thank you," Evie whispered, her gratitude a tangible force that bound them together in the cool expanse of the workshop. They stood among the tools and parts, three people united by more than just a fight against corruption.

"Shall we celebrate this new chapter?" Nate suggested, the atmosphere lightening.

"Only if we're riding there on that," Evie pointed at the motorcycle, a sly grin appearing.

"Deal," Amy laughed, "but only if you're driving."

"Challenge accepted," Evie said, her laugh mingling with theirs, the sound echoing off the walls—a chorus of hope and camaraderie in the face of life's next adventure.

Evie's fingers traced the cool, smooth surface of her new kitchen counter, a stark contrast to the rickety table that once occupied the space. Her gaze swept over the fresh paint on the walls, the hue a soothing seafoam green that Nate had suggested would bring tranquility. She inhaled deeply, the scent of lemon polish and the faintest hint of rosemary from the potted herb garden in her windowsill mingling together like an olfactory testament to her newfound freedom.

"Can you believe this place?" Evie asked, the awe still fresh in her voice. She leaned against the counter, her eyes brimming with unshed tears.

Nate leaned beside her, hands tucked in his pockets, looking around with a quiet pride. "I can," he said. "You've done wonders with it."

Amy stood by the doorway, observing the transformation not just of the space, but of Evie herself. "It's not just the place that's changed," she noted, her keen eyes missing nothing.

Evie let out a shaky laugh, a sound that carried the weight of her journey. "I used to dread coming home," she confessed, her hand now gripping the edge of the counter as if anchoring herself to the moment. "But you—you both turned it into a refuge."

"Hey, we might have given a nudge here and there," Nate replied, his tone deflecting the gravity of his deeds. "But you're the one who made it all happen."

"Still," Evie continued, her gaze locking with Nate's, then Amy's, seeking them out as if they were her lifelines. "The nights I spent feeling trapped, thinking I had no way out... You cut through that darkness. You showed me there was light." Her voice broke, thick with emotion.

"Not just light, Evie," Amy interjected, moving closer. "A whole damn sunrise."

Nate chuckled, the sound a soft rumble. "And trust me, the view from here? It only gets better."

"Promise?" Evie asked, her voice small but fervent.

"Promise," Amy affirmed, her hand reaching out to squeeze Evie's shoulder. "We're with you, every step of the way."

"Thank you," Evie breathed out, her gratitude enveloping them like a warm blanket. "For believing in me when I couldn't."

"Belief is easy when you're staring at proof," Nate said, tilting his head toward her, a teasing glint in his eye. "Especially proof as stubborn and brave as you."

"Brave doesn't quite cover it," Amy added, sharing a conspiratorial glance with Nate. "Badass is more like it."

"Badass," Evie repeated, the word foreign yet fitting on her tongue. A small smile tugged at the corners of her mouth, the first bloom of self-recognition.

"Exactly," Nate nodded, his affirmation final. "Now, how about we make some dinner in this fancy new kitchen of yours? I'm dying to see if these culinary skills you've been bragging about are as sharp as your wit."

"Challenge accepted," Evie retorted, wiping away a lingering tear before moving to the fridge with renewed purpose. "But fair warning, I set the bar pretty high."

"Wouldn't expect anything less," Amy said, joining them at the counter, ready to chop, stir, or taste whatever Evie decided to whip up.

Together, they stood in the heart of Evie's sanctuary, three souls bound by resilience and a shared resolve to keep fighting, keep thriving, no matter what shadows loomed beyond the safety of those newly painted walls.

The kitchen erupted in laughter as Evie's attempt to flip a pancake sent it flying onto Nate's head like a flat, doughy hat. "I think you missed the pan, chef," Nate quipped, plucking the pancake off his hair with an exaggerated wince.

"Hey, I'm making art here," Evie defended, her eyes dancing with mirth. "Edible art that apparently prefers Nate's company."

Amy chuckled, snapping a photo of Nate's bemused expression. "Don't worry, this is going straight to the 'Remember When' collection," she said, her voice warm with affection.

"Great, just what our album needed—more blackmail material," Nate deadpanned, but he was grinning, sharing a look with Evie that said he wouldn't have it any other way.

Evie glanced at the pair, her heart swelling at the ease of their banter. They were a team—a trio now—and it felt like they could take on the world together. She flipped another pancake, this one landing perfectly in the pan. "Second time's the charm," she muttered, a sense of accomplishment threading through her veins.

"Speaking of charms, remember our little victory at the courthouse?" Amy asked, leaning against the counter. "That was all you, Evie. You walked in there like you owned the place."

"Owned? More like borrowed it for a terrifyingly public moment," Evie confessed, the memory sharp and empowering. It was one thing to survive; it was another to stand tall in the aftermath.

"Terrifying or not, you did it," Nate said, his voice serious now. "And speaking of doing things, I think it's time we marked the occasion properly." He glanced between the two women, a conspiratorial gleam in his eye.

"Marked how?" Evie asked, curiosity piquing.

"Day trip. Just the three of us," Amy suggested, her green eyes sparkling. "We've been cooped up strategizing and plotting for too long. Let's go somewhere with no agenda."

"Somewhere with fresh air, open spaces... maybe even a beach?" Evie ventured, the thought sending a thrill through her. A beach meant freedom, the kind she hadn't felt in ages.

"Beach it is," Nate confirmed, wiping his hands on a dish towel before tossing it over his shoulder like a mock cape. "Operation Seaside Serenity is underway."

"Operation Seaside Serenity?" Evie repeated, her laugh bubbling up again. The name was ludicrous and yet so fitting for their little band of misfits.

"Hey, every good mission needs a solid name," Amy pointed out, nudging Evie playfully. "Besides, it's about celebrating. You, us, this new chapter."

"New chapter..." Evie echoed softly, her gaze drifting out the window to where the city thrummed with life. It had tried to break her, but here she stood, flipping pancakes and planning beach trips, surrounded by two people who had seen her at her lowest and had helped lift her higher than she ever imagined.

"Let's do it," she declared, conviction surging. "Operation Seaside Serenity is a go."

"Then it's settled," Nate announced, clapping his hands together. "Tomorrow, we chase the horizon."

"Chase the horizon," Amy repeated, nodding solemnly as if sealing a pact. "And leave the shadows behind."

"Leave them behind," Evie agreed, feeling the weight of the past lessen with each shared smile and promise of adventure. They were more than survivors; they were warriors basking in the spoils of their battles, looking forward to the peace that lay ahead.

"Alright, warriors," Nate said, the playful edge returning to his voice. "Let's finish these pancakes before they become sentient and seek revenge."

"Sentient pancakes," Evie mused aloud, the absurdity grounding her. "Now there's a concept."

"Only the best for our celebration," Amy added, her laughter mingling with theirs as the morning sun cast a warm glow over the breakfast nook, illuminating the start of something beautiful.

Evie stood at the edge of the cliff, the expansive ocean spreading before her like a canvas of infinite possibilities. The sharp, salty tang of the sea mingled with the crisp air, invigorating her senses. She breathed deeply, her chest expanding with more than just oxygen—hope swelled within her, buoyant and uncontainable.

"Look at that view," she said, turning to Nate and Amy, her voice a melody of wonder and excitement. "I never thought I'd see anything so beautiful."

"Freedom suits you, Evie," Nate replied, his eyes reflecting the same azure hues of the waters below.

Amy linked arms with them both, her smile radiant in the sunlight. "We've got the whole world ahead of us. This is just the beginning."

Their laughter echoed over the cliffs, intertwining with the cries of distant gulls. For Evie, each chuckle was a note in a symphony of liberation—a sound she would compose into the soundtrack of her new life.

"Remember when we could only dream of days like this?" Evie mused aloud, reminiscing yet not longing for what had been.

"Those dreams are our reality now," Amy said, squeezing her hand reassuringly.

"Let's make a pact," Nate proposed suddenly, his tone brimming with conviction. "We live every day like it's a gift because, damn it, that's exactly what it is."

"Agreed," they chorused, their voices a united front against any remnants of despair.

With purposeful strides back toward the car, Evie reveled in the solid earth beneath her feet, the sense of direction her steps took. She couldn't help but glance back once more, etching the panorama into her memory—the untamed waves, the unbroken horizon, the promise of tomorrow.

"Hey, Evie," Nate called out, interrupting her reverie. "You ready to plan our next grand escapade?"

"More than ready," she confirmed, her heart pounding a fierce rhythm of anticipation.

"Good," Amy chimed in, her gaze alight with mischief. "Because Nate's been dying to try skydiving, and I think it's about time we took the plunge."

"Skydiving? Really?" Evie's laugh carried a lilt of disbelief and thrill. "Now there's a leap of faith."

"Exactly," Nate said with a grin. "And we'll do it together."

As the trio piled into the car, Evie found herself caught up in the energy of her companions, the synergy of their shared resolve. They were more than a team; they were a family bonded not by blood, but by the trials they had overcome and the triumphs they celebrated.

"Thank you, Nate, Amy," Evie whispered, her words barely audible over the hum of the engine. "For everything."

"Hey, no thanks needed," Amy replied, meeting Evie's eye in the rearview mirror. "We're in this together, remember?"

"Always," Nate affirmed, placing a supportive hand on Evie's shoulder.

The car sped away from the cliffside, leaving behind the echoes of the past and racing towards a future ripe with potential. Evie leaned back in her seat, the corners of her mouth lifting into a contented smile. With Nate's unwavering support and Amy's infectious energy, she felt invincible. She could conquer any obstacle that came her way, always pushing forward with determination, always striving for greater heights. She was an unstoppable force, carving her own path through the unknowns of life.

Chapter 10

The dust had barely settled on the battlefield of wits when Nathaniel "Nate" Everhart and his wife, Amelia "Amy" Everhart, emerged victorious. Their latest exploit—a meticulously crafted ruse—had not only stripped Sebastian Blackwood of a significant portion of his ill-gotten gains but had also delivered justice to the long-suffering Evie Brooks. The clever couple had danced their way through a minefield of deceit, sidestepping traps with grace and smarts, and now, they watched as the fruits of their labor brought light back into Evie's eyes.

"Feels good, doesn't it?" Nate murmured, his voice tinged with pride as he leafed through the morning paper at their dining table. No headline screamed of their silent triumph, no article hinted at how a corporate shark had been outmaneuvered. It was all beneath the surface, hidden from view, just the way they liked it.

"Better than good," Amy replied from across the table. She raised her mug in a quiet toast to their success, her eyes glinting with satisfaction that could rival the sun's rays piercing through the window. "To think, that sleazeball Blackwood thought he was untouchable."

"Untouchable," Nate scoffed, folding the newspaper with a snap. He stood up and walked over to the sink, rinsing his mug with the precision of someone who knew the value of leaving no trace.

Amy watched him move about the kitchen, admiration lacing her gaze. There was something about returning to the mundanity of their daily lives that made their victories taste even sweeter. Here, in this quiet space, they were just another suburban couple. But behind closed doors, they were champions of the unseen, defenders of the downtrodden.

"Back to the grind tomorrow?" Nate asked, leaning against the counter with an ease born of countless mornings spent in this very spot.

"Yep, I've got a meeting with the editor first thing," Amy said, referring to her day job at a local news outlet. "Got to keep up appearances. And you?"

"Client's got a server issue. Can't wait to dive into that mess," he replied, his tone dripping with sarcasm. Yet, there was an undercurrent of contentment. These simple tasks anchored them, gave them a cover for their less conventional pursuits.

"Sounds exciting," Amy chuckled, her laughter filling the room like music. She paused, her expression sobering as she caught Nate's eye.

"But seriously, do you ever wonder if we should stop? What we do... it's not exactly without risks."

"Every day," Nate admitted, pushing off from the counter to sit beside her once more. "But then I remember Evie's face when she realized she wouldn't have to suffer anymore because of that bastard. That's what keeps me going."

"We're making a difference," Amy said, her voice firm, resolute. "In a world filled with bastards like Blackwood, someone's got to tip the scales back in favor of the little guy."

"Speaking of which," Nate began, a mischievous glint appearing in his eye, "I've been thinking about what our next case could be."

"Already?" Amy laughed, but the spark of excitement in her eyes matched his own. "You really can't help yourself, can you?"

"Helping ourselves isn't the point," Nate replied, his smile widening. "It's about helping those who can't fight back."

"Then let's make sure we win all our fights," Amy said, reaching for Nate's hand and squeezing it with conviction.

Nate nodded in agreement, feeling the familiar surge of adrenaline at the prospect of a new challenge. They were a team, bound by love and a shared desire for justice.

***

Nate's eyelids fluttered open to a sliver of sunlight that had muscled its way through the curtains, casting a warm glow over the room. The chirping of birds outside dovetailed with the gentle hum of suburban life awakening, a soothing counterpoint to the adrenaline-fueled nights of their recent past.

He stretched, muscles uncoiling, a far cry from the tense readiness required in their line of work. No bug-out bags needed today; no encrypted messages to decode. Just the softness of their bed and the stark fact that, for now, they were Nathaniel and Amelia Everhart, not the cunning architects of justice.

Nate padded down the hallway where the sound of sizzling and the comforting scent of coffee coaxed him awake.

Amy stood at the stove, her red hair tied back in a loose ponytail, deftly flipping an omelet in the pan. "Coffee's ready," she announced without turning, her tone light but carrying an undercurrent of shared understanding – a reassuring lack of need for disguise, just the raw intimacy of two partners who'd seen the depths of each other's souls.

"Smells like heaven," Nate replied, approaching her to peck a kiss on her cheek before settling at the kitchen table. He poured himself a mug of the dark liquid, the steam curling up into the air like the remnants of a vanishing specter.

"Sleep well?" Amy asked, sliding the omelet onto a plate with practiced ease. Her gaze met his, holding the history of countless shared glances that communicated more than words ever could.

"Like a baby," Nate said, though the statement was lined with the irony of knowing that past missions often laughed in the face of restful sleep."

"You mean, you kept waking up and crying?" Amy smiled, bringing over plates of food and joining him at the table. "We've earned a bit of peace."

Nate nodded, tucking into the breakfast with an appetite sharpened by normalcy. Between bites, he found himself studying the domesticity of their environment, the mundane kitchen utensils, the innocuous patter of neighbors starting their day. It was easy to forget, amid the clatter of cutlery and the tranquility of suburbia, that they were anything but ordinary. But underneath the surface calm, their minds were never still, always ticking away, plotting moves on a chessboard veiled from the public eye.

"Thinking about the next play?" Amy inquired, her fork pausing mid-air.

"Can't help it," Nate confessed, chasing a piece of egg around his plate. "It's like a game of whack-a-mole. You knock one down, another pops up."

"Except our moles are swindlers and crooks with too much power," Amy added, her lips curling into a half-smile that didn't quite reach her eyes—a reflection of the gravity behind their jests.

"Exactly." Nate took a long sip of coffee, letting the bitterness center his thoughts. After all, their long-term mission was far from over.

There would always be another Sebastian Blackwood, another Evie Brooks needing justice.

"Today, we breathe," Amy declared, her declaration punctuating the morning quiet. "Tomorrow, we fight."

Nate nodded, the resolve in his voice mirroring the steel in his spine. They were soldiers in a different kind of war, armed with wit and cunning instead of guns and grenades. And as they sat there, amidst the detritus of breakfast and the familiar comfort of home, they knew the battle was just beginning.

The last bite of toast lingered on Nate's tongue, a morsel as crisp and satisfying as the closure they had provided Evie Brooks. Sunlight danced across the kitchen tiles, casting a warm glow that matched the ember of fulfillment burning in his chest.

"Remember the look on her face?" Nate asked, eyes meeting Amy's across the remnants of their morning feast.

Amy paused, a softness overtaking her features. "When we handed her Blackwood's money? It was like watching someone take their first breath after being underwater for too long."

"Exactly." Nate's heart swelled at the memory. A small victory in a vast ocean of battles yet to be fought, but significant nonetheless. In their unconventional war against injustice, it was these moments that replenished their spirit.

"We gave her life back," she continued, stacking dishes with a clink that punctuated her satisfaction.

"Freedom," Nate murmured, the word tasting sweeter than any pastry. Inside, he replayed every step of their plan, each move calculated with precision and care—like a masterful hack slicing through layers of digital deceit.

"Powerful thing, huh?" Amy said, her back turned as she filled the sink with suds. Droplets of water caught the light, shimmering like the possibilities that lay ahead for Evie.

"Empowering," Nate corrected, rising from his seat to join Amy. His hands found the warmth of the soapy water, sharing the load as they always did. "We didn't just give her justice; we gave her the control she was denied."

"Her gratitude was palpable," Amy said, passing a wet plate to Nate for drying. "But it's not why we do this."

"Never has been." The towel in Nate's hands absorbed the moisture, and he took pride in the act, simple yet symbolic of their ability to wipe slates clean. "It's about righting wrongs, tipping scales back into balance."

"Even if it's one person at a time," Amy added, locking eyes with him. Her gaze held the fire of shared purpose.

Nate placed the plate in the rack, a sense of contentment washing over him. "Sometimes, one person is all it takes to start a cascade."

"Like dominoes," Amy quipped, a playful spark igniting within the gravity of their conversation.

"Or a house of cards collapsing," Nate countered, a smirk tugging at the corner of his mouth.

"Blackwood learned the hard way," Amy observed, her voice tinged with a hint of humor over the man's downfall.

"May he's the first of many," Nate said, his words a quiet vow that resonated through the kitchen and beyond its walls.

"Here's to the fallen houses and the lives we rebuild from their rubble." Amy raised an imaginary glass, her gesture solemn yet hopeful.

Nate mirrored her salute, his heart thundering a promise to the unseen faces waiting in the shadows for someone to champion their cause. "To justice," he affirmed, knowing this was far more than a toast—it was a creed by which they lived, breathed, and would continue to fight.

Acknowledgements

You.

Thank you for getting this far. This is my first novel, so perhaps it's a little "raw". I've learned from my mistakes and the next book in the series will be better. Thank you for bearing with me on this one.

Mel.

I honestly couldn't have finished this without her. Mel has been fantastic editing the first draft. She is one of the most fascinating people I have ever known and I'm both grateful and humbled to consider her a friend.

Amanda & Jackie.

I was trying to hide that I was at a bit of a low and happened to mention that I was considering writing a novel. There was a surprisingly emphatic "I'll read it" and a "Me too, I'd love to". That really cheered me up and forced me to actually start and complete this book.

NaNoWriMo.

Every year for several years, I'd loosely considered shooting for this ... and been disappointed in myself each time. The timing worked out well this year.

Milton Keynes UK
Ingram Content Group UK Ltd.
UKHW012235050124
435526UK00001B/33

9 798223 089520